# HUNGER

HELLISH #5

CHARITY PARKERSON

--Warning: This book is intended for readers over the age of 18.

Copyright © 2018 Charity Parkerson
Editor: Hercules Editing and Consultants
Photographer: Viergacht_42431
ISBN: 978-1-946099-32-7

❀ Created with Vellum

# INTRODUCTION

BLEIDD HATES EVERYTHING ABOUT EVAN, EXCEPT THE
THOUGHT OF HAVING HIM IN HIS BED.

Four years ago, a prince of Hell wiped out Evan's entire wolfpack, leaving him alone. At first, he tried fitting in with the Swedish pack, but its leader, Bleidd, banished him. Evan's crime—Bleidd's attraction to him. Now Evan is the wolf protector of a god's mate. The title puts him leagues above Bleidd. Still, the pretentious Swedish alpha turns his nose up at Evan in every way, except when it comes to trying to lure Evan to his bed.

Brought to life by Odin, Bleidd is older than Evan can fathom, much too old to play games with such a young pup. But there's something about Evan, something that keeps Bleidd coming back. When Bleidd turns up in New Orleans, he can't tell Evan the reason he's there, but he can use the trip to try to win the childish wolf he can't shake. Unfortunately for Bleidd, he's not the only creature set on having Evan. He'll have to step up his game and—more importantly—stay alive if he hopes to call Evan his mate.

# 1

---

Two weeks ago, Öland forest, Sweden.

Evan loved and hated being here. Sweden was one of the most beautiful places on earth. The air was clean. Everything smelled crisp. Unlike New Orleans, where everything stank, Evan was free to be himself here. He could change between man and wolf as he liked—no witnesses. But it was lonely in Sweden. Four years ago, the local pack leader Bleidd had banished him because Evan didn't fit in. Cohesiveness meant survival in packs. Evan wasn't working out. Mostly, it was due to the alpha's attraction to Evan. At least, that was what Evan liked to tell himself. Bleidd Gunnolf was responsible for keeping the pack strong. Evan was a wrench in the works. He'd been thrown away—like trash with no feelings whatsoever.

Since then, Evan had moved on. Goddess Celeste had assigned him to watch over a god's mate. It was an honor. Evan took his duty seriously. Thankfully, Baptiste was amazing. It wasn't hard to stick by his side. Sweden was hard. Beautiful but painful. Baptiste had brought Evan here to enjoy the full moon. Evan was trying. The knowledge that Bleidd was out there, possibly miles or maybe only yards away, ate at Evan's mind every second. He swore he could feel the man's amber-colored stare upon him. Evan didn't know why he craved the silver-haired alpha. He'd met other men. Other wolves. No one else had tempted him in the least. Evan was content alone. Most of the time. Something about knowing Bleidd was nearby brought out a restlessness inside Evan. He wasn't sure he liked it.

Evan could've played in the woods all night with the moonlight caressing his fur. Being in wolf form made his cravings too intense. That was why he'd rejoined Baptiste on the cabin's porch ten minutes earlier. He'd transformed back into a man, trying to shake off the maudlin mood that was overtaking him. Baptiste had left Evan a blanket so he wouldn't have to sit there in the nude. Evan kept the soft material wrapped around him like a shield, hoping it would keep his heart safe.

"Did you have fun?"

Evan turned sideways at Baptiste's question and leaned his back against the railing. Even though he faced Baptiste, where the man stayed hidden beneath a cloak of magic from everyone but Evan, Evan's gaze stayed locked on the nearby trees. "I don't know that 'fun' would be the word I'd use. Mostly, I just walked around, enjoying the silence. Everyone here knows Bleidd banished me, so you know. It's awkward." He almost hated being honest with Baptiste because he knew Baptiste wished to make things better. Evan felt the same about Baptiste's recent problems with his mates. It was hard to pretend he didn't notice the tears Baptiste shed.

"I'd hoped Bleidd learning you are my guard would ease your way with the local wolves."

Evan shrugged. He didn't want Baptiste to think he didn't appreciate everything he'd done. "It might. I steered clear of the other wolves."

"You're incredibly brave to come here and be the lone wolf," Baptiste said, bringing Evan's gaze his way. "They need each other. You need no one. They'll never know your depth of strength. You should be proud."

Before Evan could respond, letting Baptiste

know how much the man's words meant to his soul, a familiar scent in the air had his gaze shooting toward the tree line. He moved to his feet. Bleidd stepped into view, wearing nothing, as usual. Evan's gaze ate up the sight of silver hair, amber eyes that reflected the moon, and a body that would make Adonis jealous.

"Jeez. This guy again," Baptiste bitched, forcing Evan to bite back a smile.

"I need to speak with Baptiste," Bleidd said as he moved to a step below Evan, making them the same height. Since Evan wasn't short, that was saying something.

"He's not accepting visitors tonight," Evan said, keeping his voice hard against Bleidd. The alpha's presence always pissed Evan off every bit as much as it took his breath away.

Bleidd glanced around as if searching for any sign Baptiste might be near. His gaze moved back to Evan. His tone softened. "Listen, about earlier, I was just surprised to see you."

Evan looked away and focused on some point over Bleidd's shoulder. He'd like to say something smartass about seeing Bleidd earlier in the day when the alpha had cruelly reminded him of his banishment from the Swedish pack. "I'm sure." Even Evan heard the pain in his voice.

"I'm a leader here."

"Yep," Evan said, this time managing a disinterested tone. "I'm aware."

"It's my duty to keep the pack strong."

Evan rocked back on his heels. "So you've said."

Bleidd didn't let up. "I have great, great, great grandchildren older than you."

"That's nice," Evan said, looking away. He didn't need a reminder of their age difference.

Bleidd shifted closer, nosing at Evan's neck.

Evan flattened his palm against Bleidd's chest and pushed. He couldn't take Bleidd touching him. It hurt his heart too badly. "I'm not accepting visitors tonight either."

"You smell different," Bleidd said, not budging. "Like the city."

"What do you want, Bleidd?" Evan asked, letting his hand slip away from Bleidd's chest, stealing an extra feel of the man's hard chest and abs as it fell away.

"I saw that," Baptiste said with a chuckle. His magic shield kept Bleidd from hearing. Evan chose to ignore him.

Bleidd took a step back. "I have a message for Baptiste from the Americas king."

Baptiste tossed off his magic, revealing his presence. "What's the message?"

Bleidd's gaze moved to where Baptiste sat in a nearby chair. He didn't look surprised to see him. "Eirik and Kallus have been taken into custody. Your presence is requested."

"What?" Evan said, more than a little surprised. Baptiste's blood mate, Eirik, was a god. He should be above such things.

"I'm not sure that's actually legal, to be honest," Baptiste said, sounding as confused as Evan felt. "Since Eirik is a god, I wouldn't think Jonathan has any authority over him. I mean, Celeste—"

"Has authorized their detainment," Bleidd said, cutting Baptiste off.

"What?" Evan repeated, wishing Bleidd's claims would make sense.

"I'll go," Baptiste said, proving that even angry with his mates, he would race to their rescue.

Evan wrapped his blanket tighter around his waist. Wherever Baptiste went, he would go too. "I'll go with you and watch your back."

Baptiste shook his head. "Stay. Enjoy the night. This won't take long. An hour, at most."

Even though it didn't make sense, a flash of fear raced through Evan. Everyone left him. It would kill him if Baptiste disappeared and never returned. When he spoke, his fear laced every syllable. "Okay."

As if Evan was still in wolf form, Baptiste stroked Evan's hair, making his panic fall away. "Don't worry. I'll be back soon."

Evan nodded, and Baptiste disappeared. With nothing left to distract him, Evan was hyper aware of being alone with Bleidd. "Baptiste will sort this out," Evan said, confident in Baptiste's abilities. The Druid was strong. Strong enough to capture the hearts of a god and a demon. Dealing with Jonathan would be a snap.

"Looks like it's just the two of us," Bleidd said, sounding entirely too seductive for someone who hated everything about Evan's existence.

Evan tried looking at everything except Bleidd. "Seems so."

Bleidd's stare bored into Evan's skin. "The moon is still full."

"Yep." Why wouldn't the pack leader go away?

"We should fuck."

At Bleidd's suggestion, Evan's gaze snapped to Bleidd's. The wolf was one hundred percent serious. Evan swallowed. "Yes. We should." God help him.

He had no idea where he got the courage to answer. All he knew was—he couldn't let this moment pass or he'd never forgive himself. Bleidd had been his biggest obsession since he'd longed for the alpha before his banishment. They'd shared one kiss in the past. Then, Bleidd had booted him from the pack. Evan had never forgotten that kiss.

Bleidd took a step toward him. Evan fought the urge to take one back. His insides shook. Bleidd snagged the blanket wrapped around Evan's waist and hauled him forward. All his nervousness fled the moment their skin met. The blanket slithered to the ground. Hunger clawed at Evan's insides. He didn't wait for Bleidd to make the next move. His lips found Bleidd's.

Bleidd's body jerked, as if surprised by Evan's boldness. Despite Bleidd being the one who made the suggestion, Evan still expected the pack leader would push him away. He stood stiff beneath Evan's touch. Evan almost gave up. The instant he decided to back away, Bleidd's arms locked around him like a vise, holding Evan in place. Bleidd turned his head away. His teeth found Evan's earlobe.

"You're very oral."

It was an odd thing for Bleidd to say, in Evan's opinion. He rolled with it. "I like the way you taste."

Bleidd's tight hold turned into a caress. "I don't like to kiss."

This wasn't going well. Evan felt out of his league and ill-equipped to deal with Bleidd. Before he could decide what to say or how to react, Bleidd palmed his cock, replacing Evan's discomfort with lust. He didn't have time to cling to any newfound footing. Bleidd turned Evan in his arms and shoved him against the porch railing. Evan clung to the wood, trying to recapture his bearings. Bleidd pumped at Evan's cock, keeping him high on desire. The huge alpha sank his teeth into Evan's shoulder, and the world narrowed to a pinpoint. Evan couldn't draw a full breath. Bleidd was everywhere, overwhelming Evan with his size and power. Evan couldn't keep up. He wanted to do something, anything that would ensure Bleidd never forgot him after tonight. Evan was helpless in Bleidd's hold. The man had him caught in passion's web.

Bleidd's tongue swiped Evan's shoulder where he'd bitten him only moments earlier. Evan fought not to let his eyes fall closed at the sensation. He was already overwhelmed. Bleidd licked a path from Evan's shoulder to his neck before swiping at the shell of Evan's ear. "Mhmm, delicious. I can practically taste the innocence on your skin."

Horror raced through Evan. Was there a way he could tell? Bleidd was the expert here. Maybe there was a way he could tell.

Bleidd leaned to the side, as if trying to see Evan's reaction to his claim. "Your silence is telling. How have you managed to stay a virgin this long?"

Evan wished he had his blanket back. He couldn't remember the last time he felt this exposed. "I'm only twenty-one." Even to Evan's ears, he sounded breathless. "And I've been separated from wolves since you kicked me out. Before that, my family had just died. Plus, I don't really fit in anywhere." Evan snapped his teeth together before he admitted anything else horrifying—like the time his mom caught him masturbating. This night had taken an awkward turn. He didn't like it.

"I wish you would've said something sooner," Bleidd said as he bent and snagged the blanket before handing Evan his wish and wrapping the blanket around him. "It's not in my nature to touch an innocent or someone so young. I didn't realize."

Evan prayed Bleidd would stop talking and leave him be. It didn't happen.

"I hope you understand I only wished for a release of pent-up energy from the full moon. Nothing more."

It took some digging—deep digging, but Evan managed a bland smile. "Of course. My home is with Baptiste. Goddess Celeste chose me as his protector." Take that, fucker. Really, though. He should've known this would happen. Nothing good ever happened to him, especially when Bleidd was involved.

"Did she?" Bleidd asked, sounding skeptical. "Or did the Goddess choose Baptiste to protect you?"

The air left Evan's lungs. He'd officially been fucked in every way tonight except the way he wanted. Evan held the blanket tighter as if he could protect his heart. Jonathan appeared in a flash of light, saving Evan from what had quickly become a horrible situation. He looked between them as if surprised to see Evan wasn't alone. Evan felt sure it was beyond obvious they were arguing. Jonathan didn't make things worse. He focused on Evan. "Baptiste sent me to fetch you. Do you need to grab anything?" His gaze slid down Evan's body. "Like clothes?"

Evan shook his head and transformed into a wolf, leaving the blanket behind. He kept his gaze turned away from Bleidd as he pressed against Jonathan's legs. The world went black as Jonathan flashed them from Sweden to New Orleans in an instant, leaving Bleidd behind without a word. As the familiar scent of the bayou filled Evan's nose, he fought against the pains in his chest. If there was any mercy in the world, Evan would never see Bleidd again.

## 2

---

Present day, New Orleans.

Baptiste was one of the strongest Druids on the planet. Evan felt blessed to be his wolf, especially since Baptiste was teaching him magic. There were several spells Evan would never be able to perform since he didn't possess a single drop of magical blood. But there were other spells, plant-based enchantments powered by nature, that Evan could learn. Baptiste also owned a popular Voodoo shop inside the French Quarter. Evan worked the register in his spare time. He had a lot of free time. Since they weren't especially busy today, Evan wasted the day away by reading one of Baptiste's many spell books. To most people, it would probably be boring as hell. Evan loved going down the lists of ingredients and watching the pieces come together to create something amazing. Things he never would've realized on his own made perfect sense when he saw the spells written in Baptiste's scrawled hand.

Learning magic gave Evan a sense of purpose, especially since Baptiste had worked things out with Eirik and Kallus. Baptiste didn't really need Evan any longer. Thankfully, Odin had declared Evan Baptiste's wolf companion, giving him a reason to stay. Baptiste was happy. Evan lived side by side with their love, feeling lost and empty. He'd never be part of a pack. Evan was cool with that. He didn't fit in with wolves. Being Baptiste's wolf was better. Loneliness still found him. Thoughts of Bleidd continued haunting him. Humiliation owned him every time he thought of the wolf's rejection. Evan's vision blurred as he stared down at Baptiste's notes. When would the memory of Bleidd turning him away fade?

*Are you okay?*

Evan blinked rapidly at Baptiste's mental inquiry. *Yes. Don't worry over me.*

*Fuck that. I'm on my way.*

A mental growl rang through Evan's head. The only downside to being connected to Baptiste was that he couldn't hide anything from him. Baptiste should be enjoying time alone with his mates, not coming to hang out with Evan at the shop.

A shadow fell over Baptiste's notes, bringing Evan's head up. He knew Baptiste could travel at the blink of an eye, but he'd hoped, since the house was right behind the shop, Baptiste would walk and give him a minute to gather his strength. It wasn't Baptiste's light green gaze staring back at him. For a moment, Evan's brain couldn't come to terms with what his eyes showed him. He'd never seen Bleidd fully clothed. Bleidd's silver hair was slicked back, showing off his flawless features. Evan had no clue how old Bleidd was. There weren't any telltale lines marring the man's face to give a clue, but Evan knew the man was older than Evan could fathom. His amber-colored eyes stood out brighter than usual as he eyed Evan as if waiting for Evan's reaction. Evan couldn't stop taking in every detail— from the man's black and white flannel shirt and dark jeans to his military-style work boots. Goddamn. He was gorgeous. Evan hated himself for noticing.

"Bleidd," Baptiste said behind Evan, yanking Evan from his blatant inspection. "I wasn't aware Eirik summoned you."

Bleidd's gaze shifted from holding Evan's stare to

where Baptiste stood. He gave Baptiste a short bow. "He didn't. I'm here to see Evan."

"Nope," Baptiste said, snapping his fingers. Bleidd disappeared. Evan blinked at the spot where Bleidd stood only moments earlier. An unexpected laugh rose in his throat. Evan covered his mouth to keep it from escaping. "There," Baptiste said with a chuckle. "Let's see how long it takes him to get back from Sweden."

His amusement couldn't be held at bay. A snort escaped Evan a half second before a bark of laughter filled the air. Wolves couldn't travel the way of vampires. If Bleidd wanted to see Evan, he'd either have to find a vampire to transport him to New Orleans or fly like a human. Evan wondered which Bleidd had chosen the first time around. Flights from Sweden to the US weren't cheap. At the thought, evil satisfaction roared through Evan.

Baptiste wrapped his arms around Evan and held on, taking away his earlier dissatisfaction with life. "It's a good thing I came when I did. Is Bleidd's arrival why you're sad today?"

Only Goddess Celeste knew how badly Evan wanted to lie and claim he wasn't unhappy. "I was just thinking too much. It won't happen again."

Baptiste gently turned him, forcing Evan to meet

his gaze. He ran his fingers through Evan's hair, making Evan's eyes fall closed. Baptiste always treated him as if he was in wolf form. Evan loved it. It was all the affection he got from anyone. Otherwise, no one touched him. "Stop acting like a martyr. You have thoughts and feelings like everyone else, and you're entitled to them. So talk to me."

"Really. It's nothing. It'll pass."

"Always the stoic warrior," Baptiste said with a sigh. "Suffering in silence. All men are alike."

"I know I'm not a warrior," Evan said, feeling the need to be honest. "You don't have to placate me. When Eirik died, I was the first person Goddess Celeste encountered. That's the only reason she reanimated him in my image. If it hadn't been an emergency, we never would've met. She never would've chosen me. That doesn't make me a warrior. It makes me convenient. Not that I'm complaining," Evan tacked on, because he needed Baptiste to know he wanted to be there.

Baptiste stroked his cheek. "No matter the reason for Celeste choosing you, don't forget that it was actually Odin who picked you to be my wolf. If anyone would recognize a warrior, it's him."

The weight sitting on Evan's chest didn't lighten. He knew Baptiste tried making him feel better, but

Evan knew himself too well. "I don't think he chose me for that reason. You don't need a protector. In fact, you don't need me at all. You're braver than I am, and you're mated to a god."

"First off, fuck that. I absolutely do need you. You're my friend. Why do you think Odin chose you?" Baptiste asked, sparing Evan from being placated any further.

Evan shrugged. "Maybe Bleidd was right. Perhaps Odin thinks you should protect me."

Baptiste's expression turned fierce. "That guy better hope Odin didn't choose for me that reason, because he'll be the first fucker I'm going after to castrate. With that said, I honestly believe Odin knew we'd be stronger together, because we are. And, if I say you're a warrior, you are. No arguing. Now what are you working on?" Baptiste asked, glancing past him to the book on the counter. "Oh, invisibility spells. Do you want to try one out?"

Bleidd strolled through the door again before Evan could answer. "Would you let me have five minutes?"

"Nope," Baptiste said, snapping his fingers once more and sending the werewolf away. "This bastard," Baptiste growled. "He's really something else. Looks like he has a vampire on speed dial." Baptiste crossed the room to the shop's front door. He chanted under his breath and drew an invisible line across the doorway with his toe before rejoining Evan at the counter. "All right. Would you like to try a potion or an enchantment?"

Bleidd reappeared outside the door. He looked pissed. The man's slashing dark eyebrows had a deep line between them as he stormed the shop's open doorway. He hit an invisible wall and bounced backward. The wolf scrambled to stay upright. He was right back, trying to cross the threshold. His expression transformed from anger to confusion back to thunderous in a humorous series as understanding dawned. Baptiste had warded the place against him.

Evan looked away and hid a smile before clearing his throat and meeting Baptiste's eye. He didn't miss the wicked satisfaction in Baptiste's expression. "Can he hear us?"

Baptiste shook his head. "He can still see us, but he won't be able to hear a word we say. I could've made it where he couldn't look at you too. Where's the fun in that? I kind of like the idea of torturing him with the sight of your gorgeous form while he can't touch you at all. Quick, take your shirt off."

There was no holding back his laughter. "You're evil. I love it."

Baptiste winked. "I guess we'll have to try invisibility spells later. I'd hate for Bleidd to lose his show."

Evan's gaze slid back toward the door. Bleidd paced in front of the entrance, eyeing the open doorway, as if searching for a way around the warding. "He's beautiful, isn't he?" He knew Baptiste wouldn't judge him. After all, one of the man's mates was a demon. Baptiste was in no position to throw stones. Plus, Baptiste was his best friend, and they were mentally connected. He couldn't hide his thoughts even if he never gave them a voice.

Baptiste crossed the room and leaned an elbow on the counter before eyeing the doorway. "Truly, he is. It's a shame. Looks are often wasted on the vain. I imagine it takes a lot of confidence to lead an entire pack. Still, that doesn't mean he has to be an ass, and he definitely is a fucking ass."

"Yeah," Evan said absently. Evan couldn't deny Baptiste's claim. But, sometimes, he thought it wasn't that Bleidd was a complete bastard, as much as he didn't know how to let loose. The alpha was so tightly wound, he wouldn't know fun if it hit him in the face. Despite Evan's depression over all things

Bleidd, he was rarely serious. They had nothing in common beyond being wolves. Hell, as far as Evan knew, Bleidd had never touched another male before Evan. The alpha had several children and so on, but he'd never taken a mate. In so many ways, Bleidd was a mystery to Evan.

The back door opened, and Dante strolled in. The black-haired, emerald-eyed vampire even walked like the pirate he'd once been. In New Orleans, no one stood out as odd. Dante's hair flowing down his back and countless tattoos made him stand out for a different reason—he was arresting. The man wasn't traditionally handsome, but he oozed sex. Evan had never figured out what it was about the man exactly, but it only took one glance at him to know he could and would make every sexual fantasy come true.

Dante's gaze swept the shop, taking in everything. "What's going on here?" he asked the room in general, nodding toward where Bleidd angrily paced outside the warding.

Evan went back to staring at his spell book. It was bad enough Baptiste knew of Bleidd's rejection. Evan couldn't take someone as sought after as Dante knowing the truth too. Baptiste spared Evan from having to answer. "We're keeping out the riffraff."

Dante scratched his chin. "When did Bleidd Gunnolf become an undesirable?"

"When he insulted Evan *after* he tried seducing him," Baptiste said, again saving Evan from explaining one of the top five worst nights of his life.

"I never did like him," Dante said, his voice sounding more like the pirate with every word. "He's one of those all-about-duty-to-the-pack guys. Raff has some of those in his pack too. Pretentious fuckers."

Dante had been the New Orleans pack leader's lover for decades. Evan didn't mix with the New Orleans wolves, so he didn't know how they felt about their alpha sleeping with a vampire. He imagined it didn't set well with all of them. To be fair, there were vampires who looked down on wolves too. They equated a vampire and werewolf pairing as bestiality. At their hearts, they were all beasts, but whatever. Some old prejudices died hard. But Evan would like to think the New Orleans pack wasn't as old school and narrow minded. After all, they were a hodgepodge pack—filled with wolves, tigers, and all flavors of Weres.

"What brings you by?" Baptiste asked, steering the conversation into safer waters.

"We've been invited to a party at Riskel's

tonight," Dante said, passing a cream-colored envelope Baptiste's way. "A messenger just brought that by."

Evan nearly groaned. Riskel Aguillard was a Creole vampire who lived way out in the bayou. He was rich with old spice-trade money and owned a huge plantation in a place only boats could reach. Despite that inconvenience, no one missed his parties. They were more like drunken orgies, but everyone went. Since Evan had been banished from the Sweden pack, and everyone knew it, he didn't much enjoy the humiliation of a large gathering of his peers. If Dante intended to go, the New Orleans pack would be there. Fuck.

He straightened away from the counter, where he'd been pretending to read. "Is it okay if I skip this one, Baptiste?"

Baptiste's gaze moved over Evan's face before sliding to where Bleidd paced outside. A hint of sympathy touched his features as he reclaimed Evan's stare. "It might be fun. You might meet someone."

"I'd really rather not go."

Baptiste nodded. "Eirik and Kallus will go with me. You don't have to."

Before Evan had time to be relieved, Dante

zipped across the room, using his vampire speed against Evan. His labor-hardened body crowded Evan against the counter. Evan braced his palms against Dante's chest without thought. It was solid. Evan didn't miss that detail.

"You should go, poppet. There's nothing a pack of wild beasts enjoys more than the scent of innocence."

Evan's shoulders fell. Was there no secret he couldn't keep for himself? "No, thank you. I'll probably go to Jonathan's and enjoy the moon."

Somehow, Dante managed to shift closer until barely an inch separated them. "Jonathan and the rest of the Hellish are in Maine, dealing with a witch outbreak. Come play with your people," Dante cajoled as he leaned in and inhaled. "Damn, you really do smell delicious. Don't let Bleidd see your heart. Make him chase you. Give the beast a show." He met Evan's stare and weakened his knees with his overwhelming sensuality. "Let the rest of us have a shot."

Even though Evan knew Dante was only taunting Bleidd, Evan couldn't claim he was unmoved. "Okay."

Without warning, Dante cupped Evan's jaw and pressed his lips to Evan's neck. "See you there around ten," he breathed against Evan's skin before disappearing.

For a full minute, Evan stared at nothing and blinked. "Whoa."

Baptiste clapped once, snapping Evan out of his haze. "Looks like we're going to a party."

Evan swallowed and turned. "Seems so." As he made the claim, his gaze slid toward the door. Bleidd was gone. Evan shook off the disappointment that sneaked in. It was good that Bleidd left. They had nothing left to discuss.

## 3

Evan didn't bother dressing up. Despite Riskel being richer than most gods, the man wasn't the formal type. Not to mention, there was a good chance Evan would change tonight, becoming the wolf to roam the woods. Traveling with Baptiste, Eirik, and Kallus meant Evan wasn't forced to take an airboat while avoiding the snakes and gators. Being a god-appointed protector had its perks. Unfortunately, the quick travel also meant an early arrival. Only a few guests lingered outside the giant house in the center of the plantation. Baptiste spotted Riskel immediately and headed the man's way. Evan followed in his tracks, watching for any possible attack, even though he wasn't really there as a guard tonight. He wouldn't let anything happen to Baptiste.

Eirik and Kallus flanked Baptiste. Kallus was dressed in his usual dark suit, looking cool in the brutal heat. Eirik matched Evan in almost every way, down to his light-colored jeans and dark t-shirt, except the god living inside Evan's double made Eirik look twice as powerful no matter his form.

Riskel glanced their way. A bland smile touched his full lips. He stepped forward, extending a hand. "Eirik. It's good to see you, and your mates," he added, nodding toward Baptiste and Kallus. He craned his neck. His whiskey-colored gaze landed on Evan. "And I see Evan hiding back there."

Evan flashed him a small smile. "Thank you for the invite. It's good to see you, Riskel."

Without a qualm, Riskel pushed his way between Kallus and Baptiste to get to Evan. He held his hand out for Evan as he'd done for Eirik. Evan accepted. Riskel didn't let go. "Please, call me Risk. All my friends do," he said, shuffling closer and bringing Evan's hand to his lips. His gaze slid down Evan's body, making Evan wonder if he'd be the man's next meal.

Evan's tanned hand looked pale against Risk's dark skin. No matter how hard he tried, Evan couldn't tear his gaze away from Risk's whiskey stare. "I'll do that."

A heavy arm fell across Evan's shoulders, pulling his attention away, and forcing Risk back. He glanced over, finding unnaturally light blue eyes watching at him. "Fuck off, Risk. You're hogging all the good meat," Saber said without looking Risk's way.

If anyone else had referred to him as meat, Evan might've taken it as an insult. Saber Kazabil was a Weretiger. Meat to him was life. Seeing the dark-haired tiger always made Evan smile. "It's good to see you, Saber."

A feral smile stretched Saber's lips. His gaze moved down Evan's body as he took a step away. "You as well, Wolf. You're looking damn edible tonight."

Evan moved closer to Baptiste out of habit. He wasn't looking for protection. At least, that was what he told himself. "Thanks." Even Evan heard the question in his tone.

Saber winked before eyeing Evan once more like he intended to take Evan to the ground any second. "*Mhmm*. Catch you around."

"Why is everyone looking at me like I'm on the menu?" Evan whispered close to Baptiste's ear the moment the tiger moved on.

Baptiste turned his head and pressed his lips to

the shell of Evan's ear, keeping their conversation private. "Power is sexy, and you were already hot without it. But now that you're my wolf, everyone wants a taste of wolfy, protector of a god's mate." Baptiste stroked his cheek. "Roll with it, babe. You can have anyone you want, or no one at all," Baptiste added with a wink. "Don't be afraid to toy with them a little. Make them flex their muscles and earn you." With that order still hanging in the air, Baptiste swatted Evan on the ass and pushed him away, forcing him off on his own.

Evan spent some time wandering through the crowd, stopping to talk to a few familiar faces. He made sure he spoke to Raff and Dante when they arrived, but the couple quickly disappeared inside. Evan knew from experience he shouldn't venture inside. That's where people lost their inhibitions and their clothes. A flash of silver caught Evan's eyes. He searched the crowd, but nothing stood out. A glass of something dark found its way into Evan's hand. He drank with no real clue what it was. Alcohol burned his throat. Another glass replaced the empty one each time Evan tossed it back until his head spun. A familiar scent tickled his nose. Evan's fogged brain refused to latch on to the memory. He swore another flash of silver passed by just out of sight. Still, he wasn't quick enough to catch it.

With a shake of his head, Evan found a spot to stash his glass before heading down one of the many paths, leading away from the house. There were tons of alcoves and smaller buildings. Evan didn't venture toward them. Instead, he kept putting one foot in front of the other, hoping his head would clear. Evan had no clue where Baptiste had gone. He passed a few couples who'd obviously sought privacy. Evan kept moving until the sounds of the party muted and he found a stone bench at the edge of the thick woods surrounding the property. He sat and tilted his chin up to the night sky. The stars were bright here. Nights like tonight reinforced Evan's stance as a lone wolf. He wasn't sociable. Evan didn't care to mingle. All he wanted was the fresh air and open sky. With Eirik and Kallus here, Baptiste didn't need him. Not that Baptiste ever needed him. Damn. He couldn't shake Bleidd's voice. Nothing cut to the bone quite like the truth. No one had chosen him as Baptiste's protector. There wasn't enough alcohol in the world to drown out Bleidd's hateful opinion.

"May I join you?"

At Risk's appearance, Evan swallowed his irritation. He'd hoped to spend a quiet moment alone. It was Risk's party, the man's house, and a free country. Evan flashed him a smile. "Sure."

Risk claimed the empty space beside him. The short, concrete bench barely had room for both of them. Evan's gaze slid toward the man's blue-jeans-encased thighs. Risk's hands rested there. The muscles flexed in his forearms. Evan's interest grew. Baptiste's advice sounded better by the minute. He was Baptiste's wolf. He didn't need anyone else. Evan was free to play. His gaze slid higher. Evan tried eyeing the man on the sly. His gray t-shirt looked soft and clung to the man's perfect form. Risk looked like he'd been carved from marble. The man seemed fine with sitting in silence. Evan was never quiet unless he was alone.

"So... this is a nice place you have here."

"You've been here before," Risk said, pointing out the obvious.

Evan nodded. "I know, but I honestly don't think we've ever spoken. This was my first chance to tell you."

"In that case, thank you."

Evan nodded, searching for something else to say.

Before he found a topic, Risk did. "There are lots

of beautiful women here tonight. Why are you sitting out here alone?"

Evan fought the urge to blush. "I prefer my own company."

Risk's gaze moved over Evan's face, searching. "Or perhaps you prefer the company of someone not so gentle."

Evan looked away. A soft chuckle rumbled through the air. It was a sexy sound. "I can smell your innocence."

A huff escaped Evan. "Are you joking? You're the second person to say that to me today. How the hell could you possibly know that, and why does it matter? Goddess knows, I'm about tired of everyone pointing it out."

Risk didn't seem the least bit bothered by Evan's rant. His gaze hooded as he openly stared at Evan's mouth. The move had Evan falling silent. Risk's gaze lifted, meeting Evan's. He moved closer. Without warning, he leaned in and pressed his nose to Evan's neck. Evan didn't pull away. His heart sped. "I'm a vampire," Risk reminded him. "Everyone's blood has a certain scent. Yours is pure, yet wild and strong." He inhaled. Chill bumps rose on Evan's skin. "You're like a rare wine," Risk said, lightly touching his lips to Evan's pulse before moving away. "Take it as the compliment it's meant to be. Anyone would be lucky to taste you."

Evan couldn't blink. He feared he looked every bit as turned on as he was. Risk was very seductive. Evan had no words. A flash of silver behind Risk caught Evan's eye, capturing his attention. Bleidd moved in his direction. Evan stood. "Fuck. I have to go." He didn't wait around to see what Bleidd wanted or to make his explanations to Risk. Evan headed for the house, walking fast and hoping Bleidd wouldn't cause a scene. He tried smiling at everyone he passed. Even to him, the gesture felt unnatural. He looked for Baptiste without mentally calling out for the man. Ninety percent of the time, Evan already felt weak without help. He didn't need to add running to his best friend like he was running to his parent to tattle to the mix.

The fucking house was massive. Between the crowd and the maze-like hallways, Evan was lost in no time. A door to his left flew open. A woman stepped out, adjusting her dress. Evan wasn't quick enough averting his eyes. The image of Saber's more tattooed than not body still half erect was a vision Evan wouldn't soon shake. Still, he kept moving.

"Evan." The sound of Bleidd calling his name had panic rising in Evan. He searched for a place to hide. Before he could find anything, a hand covered his mouth and a hard chest molded against his back. Evan wasn't afraid. He marveled over his own reaction. Rather than lashing out, an odd desire to laugh overcame him. In a matter of seconds, Evan found himself closed away inside a dark closet.

"I could rid you of that untainted smell that has men chasing you down empty hallways," Saber said against his ear.

The temptation to laugh doubled. The scent of wild tiger and sex overcame him. All the times he'd felt out of his league with Bleidd paled in comparison to being locked away with the Weretiger.

Since Saber still covered his mouth, Evan licked his hand, hoping the tiger let him go before he suffocated.

Saber sucked in a hiss. His hand moved from Evan's mouth to his throat, holding him in place. "Oh, god. Do that to my cock. I'd give you anything."

"Didn't you get your fill with the blonde I just saw leaving here?"

A chuckle vibrated against Evan's throat a half second before Saber's teeth scraped his skin. Evan stifled a moan at the sensation. "There's no such thing. I saw your face when she opened the door. You liked what you saw."

What was it about over-confident men? Evan fucking loved it. Still, he wasn't easy. "You're reaching. I barely caught a glimpse."

"I can reach," Saber said, grinding against Evan's ass even as he cupped Evan's dick through his clothes. "Turn around. I'll give you the full show."

He was temptation's bitch. Before he gave in, the closet door flew open. A very pissed-off-looking Bleidd stared at him. A scary-sounding growl rent the air a half second before Evan found himself ripped from Saber's hold. Bleidd's vise-like grip tightened on Evan's hand as he kicked the door closed in Saber's face before dragging Evan down the hall. No one tried stopping Bleidd as he hauled Evan outside and down one of the side paths.

Evan was dead confused. Bleidd had done shitty things to him in the past—pushing him away and banishing him—but he'd never manhandled Evan before. In fact, Evan had never seen Bleidd lose his temper before now. "Why are you so angry with me?" Evan asked, trying to pull his hand away.

A very wolf-like growl escaped Bleidd. "Because you're just so goddamn naïve."

At Bleidd's barked insult, Evan found the

strength to pull away. Bleidd spun so fast Evan nearly tumbled backward when he found himself nose to nose with the pissed off alpha. Evan wanted to fight. He was hurt and angry. But Bleidd wasn't finished. "You're so fucking easy. That beast back there," Bleidd said, motioning toward where they'd left Saber behind. "He would say anything. Do anything to steal your innocence. Rather than defending yourself, as any sane being would, you're hiding in closets with him. What the fuck is wrong with you? First, you let Dante paw at you. Then, I catch you with a vampire sniffing your neck. Now, a fucking tiger."

The rage built and churned. Bleidd didn't want him. He didn't want anyone else to have Evan. Evan was damn tired of being insulted and treated like he was too stupid to live. "What the fuck is wrong with *you*?" Evan snapped, incapable of standing another second of Bleidd. "You don't want me. You don't want anyone else to have me. What the fuck do you want? There's an entire pack of wolves in Sweden who loves you. I have nothing. Was it not enough for you to steal an entire country from me? Must you have this place too? Is there no one else you can torment with your snide condemnation?" Evan's voice started as a yell and ended in a whisper. He was so goddam tired. First, he'd lost his family. Then, Bleidd had banished him. Now he was here, hounding his every move. Evan couldn't take anymore.

Bleidd's gaze moved over Evan's face. He shook his head. "It's like you don't even realize how much of a treasure you are." He took a step back, leaving Evan confused. "That night, at the cabin, I didn't want to take you like that. I wanted you to have more. No one should have their innocence stripped away while bent over the railing of a porch. But I can't make you see you're worth more than that. Go back to the beast. Let him fuck you in a closet and never think of you again. I gave up my pack to come for you. That's what I've been trying to say to you all day. I see now, it matters not at all." With a shake of his head, Bleidd walked away.

Rather than cooling Evan's temper, Bleidd's claim left him enraged. Evan chased after him, yelling at the man's back and uncaring of being overheard. "Fuck you for putting that off on me." Bleidd didn't slow. Evan didn't let up. He was furious that Bleidd would walk away from his pack. He was doubly angry the man would blame him rather than his cowardice. "I didn't ask you to leave your people. In fact, I've never asked you for a goddamn thing." Bleidd veered off into the woods. Evan followed. "I kiss you. You put me out. I kiss you again. You tell me you don't like that. I go away. You come after me. If you don't like anything about me, stay the fuck away. Go back to your pack and beg their forgiveness. Whatever you do, stop blaming me because you're too weak to be a leader *and* say I'm who you want." Evan froze. "Fuck this," Evan growled under his breath. "I'm going back to Saber. Or maybe I'll find Risk," he said to himself as he headed back toward the clearing. "Anyone who isn't ashamed of me is better than this bullshit," he spat, slapping some low hanging branches out of his way. His throat hurt. Why did he always let Bleidd make him feel worthless? Baptiste was right. There were a ton of men out there. Evan kicked at the loose dirt. He didn't need this one. Before he could break through the tree line, Evan's body lifted from the ground. His mind scrambled to make sense of why he was moving backward. Tree bark bit into his spine as his back hit the nearest tree. Bleidd's alpha status showed itself as he hovered over Evan—nostrils flaring and chest heaving. His eyes glimmered in the dark, hinting at the wolf hidden beneath human skin. Evan half expected Bleidd would bare his fangs.

A preternatural growl sounded in the man's voice

when he spoke. "You are mine." Bleidd's mouth slammed down on Evan's with enough force Evan tasted blood. His tongue shoved its way inside Evan's mouth.

Without thought, Evan bit him. When Bleidd jerked back. Evan's anger boiled to the surface once more. "You don't like kissing. So don't."

Bleidd's hand shot out. His fingers encircled Evan's throat and tightened. Evan could still breathe but not move. The man's dark expression kept Evan every bit as paralyzed as Bleidd's hold. "I want to kiss *you*," he said, leaning in once more.

Evan didn't protest as Bleidd's lips touched his. This time, Bleidd was gentle. His hold on Evan's throat became a loving caress. Their tongues brushed. For a man who didn't like to kiss, Bleidd was perfection. He took Evan's breath and scattered his thoughts. Evan clung to the alpha's shirt. His knees weakened.

Bleidd spent a moment sucking Evan's bottom lip before pulling away. He stared at Evan's mouth as he wiped the moisture from Evan's lips. "Don't go to someone else." His eyes lifted. Their gazes met. Heat and something else Evan couldn't decipher flashed in Bleidd's eyes. "Please?"

If Bleidd had ever begged anyone for anything in

his life, Evan wouldn't believe it. Yet, here he was. Evan swallowed. "Okay."

While holding his stare, Bleidd trailed his fingers down Evan's chest and stomach. When he reached the hem of Evan's shirt, his hand snaked its way beneath, stroking Evan's stomach. His fingers curled around the edge of Evan's jeans. Bleidd's gaze never wavered as he caressed Evan's skin below the waistband of his underwear "Wait for me tonight. Let me in when I come for you."

Every breath Evan took was so shallow, he could barely respond. "Okay." Damn. He was a fool, but he'd never get over the fantasy of having Bleidd until he'd had him.

Bleidd never smiled or looked the least bit triumphant. That was the only thing saving Evan's pride. Bleidd leaned in once more and touched his lips to Evan's. They shared each other's air for a moment before Bleidd backed away. "Go find Baptiste. I don't trust myself around you otherwise."

With a nod, Evan walked away. He could ignore his aching cock. After all, he'd done so for years. Evan had a hell of a time ignoring Bleidd's stare boring into his back. That was something he wanted to act on more than he craved his next breath. He'd wait. Bleidd would come. Then Evan would get the fuck over this obsession and move on.

———

BLEIDD WATCHED EVAN WALK AWAY WITH HUNGER IN his heart. He'd lived countless years. For him to say he'd never met anyone who he wanted more than he yearned for Evan made Evan beyond special. That was also why the young wolf scared the fuck out of Bleidd. There was something about him. Something behind the man's dark blue eyes. Bleidd worried he'd uncover the truth too late to save himself from whatever Evan possessed that ensnared him.

Bleidd's skin singed, making him hiss. He automatically tried shifting away from the pain, only to find himself trapped in place by the silver blade pressed against his throat.

"He really is amazing, isn't he?" Risk asked against the shell of Bleidd's ear. Helpless rage rolled through Bleidd. He'd been so engrossed in watching Evan walk away, he'd let the vampire get the drop on him. "I wonder how he'll react when he learns you're not really here for him as you claim."

"Who's to say I'm not?" Bleidd asked, brazening it out.

An evil-sounding laugh brushed Bleidd's ear. "Everyone who knows you. You should let the boy be. There are plenty of men here who'd love to own him."

That was the problem, wasn't it? "Evan doesn't need an owner. My guess is, he doesn't need anyone."

"That's good," Risk said, touching the blade to Bleidd's throat once more, burning his skin, and steering him away from where Evan disappeared. "Since you won't be making that date tonight."

Fuck. Evan wasn't likely to forgive him that. He'd known Riskel for years. Bleidd realized he'd been taking a chance by coming here. He'd gone even further by letting the vampire see him when he'd interrupted Riskel's obvious attempt to seduce Evan, but as much as Riskel despised him, Bleidd never thought the vampire would stoop to this. Bleidd had recognized the first time he'd set eyes on Evan the pup would be trouble. Back then, he hadn't expected Evan would bring him quite this much grief. There was no way he could've foreseen Evan would lead him into an attack.

## 4

W hen the sun peeked through the blinds, Evan finally accepted the truth. He'd been stood up. As much as his chest hurt, Evan wasn't all that surprised. Bleidd never missed a chance to hurt him. This would be the last. Obviously, Evan was a fool who needed to be kicked repeatedly before he learned, but he'd finally gotten the message. Kissing Bleidd that first time had been a mistake Bleidd obviously would never be finished punishing him for, but Evan was done.

He greeted Baptiste with a smile at breakfast, keeping his pain buried deep. This time, he would keep the humiliation to himself. After all, this time, he recognized he was the one to blame. Evan would kill the weakness inside him if it was the last thing he did.

Evan stared at the toaster, waiting. His gaze never wavered from the red coils singeing the bread. He was so engrossed in the process, he jumped when Baptiste stroked his back.

"Are you all right, babe?"

Evan faked a smile. "I'm fine. How are you?"

Baptiste's blond hair stood in every direction and dark circles marred his eyes. The man had obviously had a lot more fun last night than Evan. "You disappeared last night."

That was true. Evan had found Dante and had the man flash him home. He'd needed some quiet. Evan also had known if he spoke to Baptiste, the ancient Druid would see right to his soul and know he wanted to go home to wait for Bleidd. Evan had wanted his night with Bleidd to be for him alone. Well, he'd been right. He'd been completely alone the entire time.

"Dante brought me home. You know parties aren't my thing."

Baptiste eyed him while biting his lip. Finally, he obviously couldn't hold his thoughts any longer. "You'd talk to me, wouldn't you? If there was a problem?"

Guilt set in. "Of course, I—"

"For Odin's sake," Eirik said, snagging Baptiste

around the waist and heading for the table. "Leave the boy be. Come entertain me."

Evan didn't look the gift interruption in the mouth. The instant the bread popped from the toaster, Evan crammed the piece in his mouth and headed for the door. He needed to get to the shop and out from underneath Baptiste's watchful eye before the man broke him. Not to mention, he couldn't sit in a room filled with so much love. Kallus would be downstairs soon, and this place could easily fill with steam.

As Evan unlocked the shop's door and the scent of magic overcame him, he inhaled. No place smelled like the forests of Öland, but magic had a delicious aroma all its own—like endless power. Since Evan always felt weak, this place was a haven. Around six that morning, when it had truly set in Bleidd wouldn't show, Evan made a decision about the future. He would dedicate himself to learning all Baptiste could teach him. The easiest thing Baptiste had taught him so far was creating a luck poppet. Since he had an extra few minutes before the shop opened and all the ingredients needed, Evan cleared his mind and threw together a rudimentary poppet. It wasn't the prettiest of dolls, but Evan still caught himself smiling as he stared at what he'd done.

Not everyone found love. Evan had always known, in the back of his mind, he wasn't meant for the life Baptiste had, living with an overabundance of love keeping him fulfilled. Evan brushed his finger along the doll's arm. He would find happiness in other things.

"That's good. Her magic is strong."

Evan smiled at Baptiste's praise and sudden appearance over his shoulder. "I had a good teacher."

Baptiste kissed his neck and wrapped him in a tight hug. "We'll work on warding off evil spirits next. I think you need that one."

"Sounds good."

"For now, what do you say to taking the day off?" Baptiste asked while still holding tight. "I hear Jonathan came home early this morning. We could stop by for a visit and you could go all wolf-like and chase some bees."

He knew Baptiste felt the sadness Evan tried hard to hide. Evan didn't want that. "Nah. Jonathan probably doesn't want visitors the second he's home, and I got to enjoy the fresh air last night. Don't worry about me," Evan said, turning in Baptiste's arms and meeting his stare. "I promise I'm fine. I'm a Werewolf. We're moody. You just haven't gotten used to being mentally connected to all that inner drama yet."

"Are you su—" Baptiste's gaze snapped over Evan's shoulder. "Well, that's new," he said, heading for the door.

Evan turned, curious over what snagged Baptiste's attention. Risk stood outside, waiting to be let in. That was new. As far as Evan knew, Riskel rarely left the deep bayou.

Baptiste unlocked the door and waved Risk inside. "Hey. Did you not get enough of us last night?"

Risk's gaze slid Evan's way. "Not all of you."

"All righty, then," Baptiste said, visibly biting back a smile. "I'll just be over here, doing stuff..." Baptiste wandered off, inspecting the shelves on the opposite side of the room. Evan wasn't fooled. He knew Baptiste hung on every second.

"You ran away last night."

*You what? We're discussing this.*

Evan ignored Baptiste's mental push. "Yeah, sorry. I—"

"No need to explain," Risk said, cutting him off. "I saw Bleidd chasing after you."

Baptiste spun, eyeing Evan over Risk's shoulder. *You have some explaining to do.*

"Yeah. He's..." Evan didn't know how to finish that sentence.

"Determined to make your life miserable," Risk finished for him.

Evan flashed him a smile. "It would seem so."

Risk nodded. His serious expression never wavered. "I'm not surprised. Bleidd is..." Risk paused as if searching for the right word. "Relentless in his need to hurt others." Evan was taken aback by that description. At the moment, it felt apt. "But that's not why I stopped by," Risk continued, not letting Evan dwell. "You rushed off last night before I could ask if you have plans for tonight."

Evan was half a second away from toeing the ground and blushing like a twelve-year-old. Risk was hot. Doubly so with the sun hitting his dark skin, making him seem to glow. "Um." Fuck. Heat rushed to his cheeks. "I don't get off from here until six."

"Then I'll pick you up at seven."

His bottom lip was getting sore from Evan worrying at it, trying to fight his smile. "I'll be waiting."

Risk's gaze dropped to Evan's work boots before slowly making its way back to holding Evan's stare. The heat in the man's eyes nearly had Evan panting. "I'll see you then."

Evan nodded. His voice refused to work as he watched Risk walk away. He might've stared at the door all day if not for Baptiste.

"Okay. Spill. What the fuck happened last night? Bleidd was there? What the hell?"

"Hey, sexy," Kallus said, clearing the back door and saving Evan from answering.

Evan moved away, giving Kallus space to attack Baptiste, maneuvering him into a quiet corner of the store. They were cute. Evan forced himself to keep his eyes averted, choosing instead to hang out behind the counter. The bell above the door jingled, reminding Evan he'd forgotten to prop it open for the day, and bringing his head up. Saber strolled inside—low slung jeans, tight t-shirt, and leather jacket. Evan's mouth went dry at the first sight of him. Saber moved his sunglasses from his face to his head. His light-blue gaze swept the shop before landing on Evan.

One corner of Saber's mouth lifted in a self-satisfied way that weakened Evan's knees. The tiger didn't bother with hellos. "I was thinking. Maybe I came on a little strong last night."

*The list of things you forgot to tell me about last night keeps growing.*

*Worry about your man.* Evan tried to ignored

Baptiste's invasion into his mind to focus on Saber. "Just a tad."

The predatory gleam to Saber's smile should've sent all sorts of warning bells to clanging. It didn't. "Well, then," Saber said, leaning on the counter and brushing the back of Evan's hand with his finger. "Maybe you'll allow me to take you to lunch and let me try again."

Evan bit his bottom lip, tying to keep his smile in check. "I'll have to check my schedule."

"He's free," Baptiste called out, making Evan's eyes fall closed in horror.

When they reopened, he found Saber's smile had grown, but his gaze never wavered. Evan couldn't look away from the man's unnaturally light blue eyes. "What time would you like to meet?"

A soft, deadly-sounding chuckle escaped Saber as he straightened away. "The moment you're free, I'll pick you up."

"He's free now," Baptiste called out, ensuring there could be no doubt he was still eavesdropping. "I told him to take the day off but be back by five."

"That's even better," Saber said, plucking his sunglasses off his head and tucking them inside his coat pocket. "We should get going, then."

Evan spent a moment marveling over how much

he liked the alpha type. Who in their right mind liked being bossed around? Apparently, he did, because his feet moved without his brain's permission. "Okay."

Saber's gaze slid his way. The man's cocky smirk had Evan measuring each breath. "I'll have you back in time for your guardian duties." With that promise in the air, Saber headed for the door.

Evan followed. He pulled a face as he passed Baptiste and Kallus—like he was biting back a silent whimper as he motioned toward the way Saber moved. It was sexy as fuck—like a predator. Evan had a bad feeling he'd bitten off more than he could chew. Baptiste buried his face against Kallus' chest. His shoulders shook with silent laughter. Evan couldn't help it. Saber was... damn. The way his hips swung. Goddamn. Saber pulled open the door and turned, waving Evan ahead of him. Evan rearranged his features and gave the man a solemn nod of thanks as if he hadn't been openly ogling him only seconds earlier.

On the sidewalk, Evan paused, waiting for Saber. "What did you have in mind?"

Saber motioned toward a nearby motorcycle. "Do you ride?"

Evan shook his head. He watched as Saber

unhooked a second helmet from some netting. Evan didn't know anything about motorcycles. He only knew enough to recognize it was a Harley.

"I was hopeful," Saber said, holding out the helmet. "Still interested?"

A smile pulled at Evan's lips as he accepted the helmet. As he pulled it on, Saber straddled the bike and slapped a helmet on.

He glanced over his shoulder. "You coming?"

Evan fought against his nervousness as he climbed on, straddling Saber's large body. When he clasped the man's waist, Saber fired the motorcycle to life. Evan's nervousness doubled. He didn't know Saber. Not really. The tiger could be taking him anywhere.

"Don't worry. I'll take care of you."

Evan marveled over Saber's voice inside the helmet. Even though he wasn't sure if Saber could hear him too, he still responded, "I trust you."

A low chuckle rumbled through the speaker he couldn't see. "I like the sound of that." Saber pulled away from the curb, forcing Evan to wrap his arms around his waist and hold tighter to keep from flying off. Saber held his silence as he drove. Evan's mind stayed firmly locked on the body beneath his hands. At first, he tried hard to ignore the way Saber's stomach muscles rippled. He never expected someone so hard would feel so soft. Evan lost the battle against the need to stroke Saber. Under the guise of finding a more comfortable position, Evan slid his hand across Saber's abs. Fuck. The man's body was amazing. When Saber turned down a dirt road, Evan blinked in surprise. He'd been so focused on enjoying Saber's body, he hadn't taken notice of where they were going.

"What is this place?" Evan asked, eyeing the unfamiliar surroundings. The road was narrow. Moss-covered trees hung over the path, coming together on each side and creating a dark tunnel.

"You'll see."

Before Evan had time to ask any more questions, Saber turned down a barely visible drive. The trees cleared, revealing a small cabin. Evan barely spared the place a glance. The lake behind it held his attention. The sunlight glimmered off the water, making it sparkle like diamonds. Everything smelled crisp and wild. The wolf inside Evan itched to burst free and run. He was forced to measure his breath the same way he'd done while watching Saber walk. Everything about the place called to him.

"It's beautiful."

Saber pulled in next to the cabin and killed the bike. He pulled off his helmet. "It's home."

Evan removed his helmet. "Seriously? This place is amazing," Evan said, climbing from the bike.

When Saber's silence finally penetrated Evan's awe, Evan's gaze slid the man's way. He watched Evan, looking more genuine than Evan could remember ever seeing him. He seemed thoughtful. "I don't bring people here."

Evan wasn't sure why Saber told him such a thing. "Okay."

"Somehow, I knew you'd appreciate it." Saber confused Evan with his seriousness.

Evan didn't let it taint the moment. "You're right. I don't get to leave the city much any longer. Baptiste used to take me to the Öland forest in Sweden, but..." Evan thought it best to stop talking. He shouldn't talk about Bleidd while on a date with someone else.

"You were banished," Saber said, filling in the blanks. He held out his hand for Evan. Evan didn't hesitate accepting. With the slightest tug, Saber led him toward a picnic table near the water's edge. "You shouldn't be ashamed," Saber said, hanging on to Evan's hand, even as he sat backward on the bench next to Evan. "Lots of Weres came to America because they'd been cast out of clans in other countries. Look at you now. You're the guardian of a god's mate. That's huge."

Evan fought the urge to argue he wasn't a warrior. He imagined Saber could see that much for himself. Instead, he chose to explain his relationship with Baptiste. "Actually, even though Celeste appointed me as Baptiste's guardian, we're bonded by Odin. He is my family."

Saber's eyebrows rose. "Seriously? I haven't heard of that happening, since…" Saber stared into space for a moment, as if trying to remember. He shook his head. "It's been at least a few hundred years." Saber focused on him once more, making Evan's stomach knot with want. He moved closer, crowding Evan's space. "There's definitely something special about you. I'd like to get to know you. Find out what it is." Without thought, Evan's gaze dropped to Saber's full lips. Even when he wasn't smiling, Saber still looked cocky. An unexpected wave of longing overcame him. Saber smiled. "You're staring at my mouth."

"I like to kiss," Evan said before he realized what he'd done. Horror washed over him.

"Is that so?" Saber snagged Evan around the waist and had him straddling his hips before Evan knew how it happened. He braced his palms against Saber's wide shoulders while staring into the tiger's beautiful eyes, which were now only inches away. "As it happens," Saber said, sounding sexy, "I like that too. Now you know where to come," Saber said as he touched his lips to Evan's.

The world fell silent as their lips clung. Saber licked Evan's bottom lip. Passion roared through him, exploding through their kiss. Their tongues met and stroked, toying with each other. Saber massaged his back, skin on skin. Evan's breath stuttered from his lungs. He liked Saber's touch. A little too much. They didn't know each other. He was certain that didn't matter to someone like Saber. The way Saber kissed made Evan wonder if it mattered to him either. After spending a few seconds sucking on Saber's bottom lip, enjoying the man's flavor, Evan kissed a path to the man's ear. He needed to slow things down. Catch his breath.

Evan found himself sucking on the man's earlobe. His dick begged for attention. Evan's heart raced. "Damn." The word came out in a breathless pant.

Saber's hold tightened. "Agreed."

"I think we need to cool off." Even though Evan

was the one who made the claim, his hold on Saber didn't lessen.

"Agreed," Saber repeated. He came to his feet, leaving Evan unbalanced and tearing a laugh from his throat as he tossed Evan over his shoulder. "I hope you like to swim."

A shot of horror raced through Evan as he realized Saber's intentions. "No." In Evan's head, his denial sounded vehement. In truth, it came out mixed with breathless-sounding peals of laughter. Instead of tossing Evan in the water, as he'd expected, Saber walked into the lake with Evan over his shoulder—shoes, jacket, and all. Evan couldn't stop laughing. No sound emerged. His whole body shook. A half second before Saber dove beneath the water, Evan held his breath to keep from sucking the whole lake into his lungs. Beneath the water, Saber finally released him. Before he could resurface, Saber's lips found his once more. It was a quick kiss. No more than a brushing of lips. Evan's heart turned over in his chest. No one ever played with him. For as long as he could remember, he'd been trapped in a world of being dutiful all the time. Saber was different. For the first time in years, Evan felt his age.

When they came up for air, Saber whooped like a large child. He swam closer and snagged Evan around the waist, leaving him no choice but to cling to him. Saber swept Evan's wet hair away from his face. "I promised I'd have you home by five. I didn't say you'd go home unsoiled."

Evan couldn't help but wonder if there was a double meaning behind Saber's words. "Do you hear me complaining?"

While holding his stare, Saber worked Evan's shirt up until Evan raised his arms and let him have it. Saber tossed it toward the shore. His gaze turned hotter by the second. "When you start, I'll stop."

"Deal." Even Evan heard the breathless note to his voice. Fuck it. He'd been good for too long.

Saber nipped at his chin before licking Evan's throat. "Don't worry," he said against Evan's skin. "I'll let you keep that innocence that has men chasing you down hallways and yanking you from perfectly good closets."

Evan's eyes fell closed at the sensation of Saber's tongue stroking him. His grip tightened on Saber. "That's a shame."

Saber's teeth scraped Evan's shoulder. "It is, isn't it? Still, I want you to know me."

Goddamn. Evan was too turned on to care, but Saber was obviously determined. "I understand," Evan said, even though he wasn't sure he did. "Do tigers even like the water?" Evan asked, trying to turn the tides if this wasn't going anywhere.

The button on Evan's jeans came loose. Saber slid Evan's zipper down. "Oh, babe. You have no idea." Before the words completely fell, Saber was palming Evan's hard dick.

Each breath Evan took came harder than the last as he rode Saber's palm. "This isn't me complaining, but this feels at odds with your earlier claims."

Saber chuckled before his teeth sank into Evan's shoulder. Everything the tiger did turned Evan on. He was already closer to coming unglued than he'd like to admit, especially with Saber gnawing at his neck. "There's so much else we can do. You won't be disappointed." Fuck. He wasn't disappointed now. Saber would really have to work at it if he wanted to let Evan down at this point. "Are you game?"

A moan escaped Evan as Saber jacked his cock. He tried catching his breath. "Yeah, I'm game."

"Good," Saber breathed as he recaptured Evan's mouth. Evan tried concentrating on their kiss. All he could think about was the hold on his cock and the release just out of his reach. After tearing his mouth away, Evan tilted his head back and sucked air. Saber was relentless. He switched between quick strokes and light touches, teasing Evan to the point of insanity. Saber's strokes turned steady but painfully slow. "Beg me," Saber demanded against Evan's throat. "Plead with me to give you release. I want to hear your need."

Evan's chest heaved as he struggled for air. "Fuck you. I grovel for no one." Even to Evan's ears, it sounded like a lie.

"You will for me."

Saber's confidence almost had Evan ready to crawl across broken glass on his bare knees. Instead, Evan pushed Saber's hand away. "There's nothing you can do for me, I can't do for myself."

"You're wrong," Saber growled, sounding more like an animal than a man as he reclaimed Evan's cock and his mouth. The man's tongue filled Evan's mouth, taking more than he gave. His motions quickened, drawing Evan's balls up tight. Pressure built and climbed. Evan's fingers dug into Saber's shoulders as he drew closer to the edge. The world fell silent. Evan held his breath. Lights exploded behind his closed lids. Wave after wave of ecstasy shook him. Moans vibrated through their kiss.

Even when Saber turned his face away, he still didn't stop stroking Evan's dick. "Fuck," he cursed, sounding as if he'd been the one who'd been sent flying. He pressed his lips to Evan's ear. "You'll be magnificent on my cock. I already know it."

Goddamn. Evan knew it too.

---

SEVERAL TIMES, EVAN DIPPED HIS HEAD BENEATH THE water falling from the shower head to hide his blush. Damn, Saber hadn't been lying. There was so much he could do without stealing Evan's virginity. His body ached in the best of ways. He moved slower than usual. Slower than he should. His hair was still wet when Risk arrived for their date. The day had been exhausting already. Guilt was the only thing keeping Evan from canceling. The way Risk smiled when Evan stepped outside to greet him gave him another push. Before today, he'd never had any man happy to see him other than Baptiste, and he didn't count. His ego needed the boost.

"You look amazing."

Evan glanced down at himself at the compliment. His worn jeans and Henley didn't look like much to him. "Thanks. You didn't say what we'd be doing, so I didn't know what to wear."

Risk invaded his space. "You're perfect," he breathed as he wrapped one arm around Evan's waist. The world turned black. Stars whirled by until the ground beneath Evan's feet changed. They stood in the center of a dining room. Candles flickered on a nearby table. It took Evan a second to realize they were inside Risk's home. He'd only seen the dining room in passing, since he'd never been on a full tour.

Risk didn't release him.

Evan met his gaze. The man's whiskey-colored stare moved over Evan's face as if searching for something. Evan stood still for his inspection. He was oddly curious, wanting to hear all Risk's thoughts, as if the man saw what Evan could not. "Why aren't you mated?"

At the question, Evan laughed and stepped out of Risk's hold. "I'm an outcast. No one wants me."

"That's not true in the least," Risk said, moving to the table and leaving Evan wondering which part wasn't true. From where Evan stood, he was both. Risk held out a chair for Evan. "I hope you like Étouffée. It's my specialty."

"You made this?" Evan asked, accepting the seat at the table. He eyed the bowl. "This looks amazing."

"I like to cook," Risk said as he circled the table and sat across from Evan. He motioned toward the food sitting in front of Evan. "Please, eat."

Evan picked up his spoon. "Thanks. I didn't

realize how hungry I am until the smell hit me." Evan took a bite. He almost hummed. It was perfect. There was just enough spice to give it kick without sending him scrambling for water. He quickly swallowed. "Oh, wow. This is amazing."

Risk brought a glass of wine to his lips and sipped. The move didn't hide the pride in his smile. "Thank you. I admit, I don't cook as much as I used to. After a while, it becomes pointless when you live alone."

Evan took another bite. While he chewed, he looked around, taking note of the luxury surrounding them. There was a china cabinet nearby filled with pieces that cost more than most people's car. Evan knew that, and he wasn't an expert. He could smell the gold lining. His gaze shifted to the chandelier hanging above the table. Crystal. He couldn't take the curiosity. "Why do you live alone in this huge place? I don't get it."

A soft chuckle escaped Risk. "What's not to get?"

Evan couldn't decide if the vampire fished for compliments or simply didn't see what Evan saw. After taking a sip of wine, which tasted expensive, Evan leaned back and eyed Risk. "You're gorgeous," Evan said, trying to sound pragmatic rather than showering Risk with blatant flattery. "This place is amazing. You obviously know everyone. And," Evan said, leaning forward and scooping up another bite. "You're one hell of a cook. I should think people would be tripping over themselves to win you."

Risk looked away and focused on the wall. He tapped his spoon on the table. It hadn't escaped Evan's notice Risk wasn't eating. When he met Evan's stare once more, a bright smile stretched his lips. "I don't like ninety-eight percent of the people I know."

A snort escaped Evan. In that moment, Risk reminded Evan of Bleidd. Maybe not as cranky, but definitely as unbending. "Ninety-eight percent of the people you know don't like me, so I won't judge you."

"Now, that, I don't believe for a second," Risk argued with a laugh.

Evan shrugged. "I talk a lot and have too much energy. Between that and my banishment, I don't land on a lot of invite lists."

Risk smirked. "Fuck them. I want to hear all your stories."

Evan shook his head in disbelief. "You asked for it."

Risk ate while Evan talked. Occasionally, Risk threw in a tidbit to keep Evan talking, but Evan never needed much encouragement. The food disappeared. Three bottles of wine followed suit.

Somewhere in the distance, a clock chimed two, making Evan realize they'd talked for hours. He stretched, and his back popped.

Risk winced at the sound.

"Holy crap," Evan whined as every muscle in his body screamed in protest from sitting in the same spot too long.

Risk stood and held out his hand for Evan. "Come on. Let's walk off some of this wine before I take you home."

Evan's palm slid across Risk's, and the man pulled him to his feet. Hand in hand, they headed for the door. Risk held it open, letting Evan go first before linking his fingers through Evan's once more. They walked for what seemed like forever without leaving Risk's property.

"This place is huge."

Risk nodded. "But look, here's the bench where I came so close to kissing you last night."

With a chuckle, Evan sat.

Risk joined him. He brought Evan's hand to his lips. "Have I mentioned how sexy you look tonight?"

*Evan.*

Evan turned his head as the whisper brushed his mind. The familiar scent of Öland forest was back. Clear and crisp. Evan eyed the path. It became more overgrown as it went. "What's down this way?"

Risk cast a quick glance down the path. "The old slave quarters. They're falling down now. No one goes that way."

Evan focused on Risk. There was something dark in the man's tone. He tried making it better. "I guess it's a good thing I stopped here last night."

Risk's hand shot out. Evan almost jumped away at the sudden movement. Risk's fingers found the ends of Evan's hair. He toyed with the locks, wrapping them around the tip of his finger. He kept his gaze locked on his hand. "For more reasons than one, I think."

Evan had become so engrossed in watching Risk's eyes, he forgot what they were talking about.

Risk's focus shifted his way. Their gazes met. "Otherwise, I might not have gotten a moment alone with you." Risk's fingers moved to Evan's jaw. He lightly stroked.

Nervousness mixed with discomfort to run away with Evan's mouth. "Why did you want to be alone with me? I mean, I've lived here for three years, and no one has wanted anything to do with me. Now everyone is showing up at my door."

Risk didn't back down. His thumb moved to

Evan's bottom lip. He stroked. "Bleidd came here, chasing you."

"Yes," Evan said, mesmerized.

"No doubt, one of the local Weres has taken interest too."

Shock rocked Evan. "How did you know that?"

"You're a guardian wolf now," Risk explained while holding Evan's stare and wooing him with his sensual tone. "You'll soon have Weres coming from all around, hoping to win you as their mate. As the protector of a god's mate, their pack will receive a huge dowry from Odin for leaving their pack to stay with you." His gaze dropped to Evan's mouth. "But I'm a Vampire. I'll get nothing and want nothing, but you. You've grown up much sexier than I ever imagined."

In his heart, he knew Risk wanted to kiss him, but Risk had gotten in his head with his claim. If what he said was true, no one really wanted him for him. Bleidd didn't like to kiss, and Saber had only kissed him in hopes of getting some massive amount of money Evan hadn't known about. Evan doubted himself. Everyone was confusing him. Risk inched closer and dipped his head.

*Evan! Don't trust him.*

Evan turned his head, peering down the overgrown path once more. "Did you hear that?"

"The trees talk out here," Risk said, shifting to his feet. He held his hand out to help Evan stand. "I'll take you home."

A hint of disappointment wormed its way in. He had zero attention span and had ruined things with someone genuinely interested in him. Evan stood. He held tight to Risk's hand when the man tried pulling away, forcing Risk to meet his stare.

Once Evan had Risk's attention, he found his courage. "Thank you for tonight." Without waiting for Risk to respond, Evan invaded the man's space and covered his mouth with his. For a moment, Risk went still beneath Evan's touch, as if surprised by the move. Then, he deepened their kiss, brushing his tongue along Evan's. It was sweet but not heated like Saber's kiss or all-consuming like Bleidd's. Evan wondered if it wasn't the kiss he needed, though. Maybe Risk wouldn't wreck him.

*Run, Evan. Riskel is deadly.*

Evan turned his face away and eyed the path once more. He wasn't imagining things. Bleidd was in his head. Risk dragged his lips down Evan's throat, keeping his attention split. But Evan had to know. He shouldn't be able to hear Bleidd's thoughts, but there was that one time when Bleidd had heard Evan's. Evan held Risk's head between his hands and tilted his chin up, giving the man better access. With Risk distracted, Evan concentrated on the rugged path and projected his thoughts as he did while mentally conversing with Baptiste.

*Where are you?*

*Riskel has me bound in silver. I'm weak. It's dark. Can't see.*

Bleidd's voice sounded fainter by the second. Evan tried processing what he'd heard. He wasn't losing his mind. Bleidd was reaching out to him. Risk's fangs scraped Evan's pulse.

Evan stepped back, pulling away. "Sorry. I can't—"

Risk looked beyond turned on and Evan nearly groaned. Bleidd hadn't shown himself as trustworthy. Evan loved having someone look at him the way Risk was now, but if Bleidd was telling the truth, Evan needed to get out of there. "You're right," Risk said, cutting him off, sounding more like an animal than a man. "I have no right. You're a guardian. That's a position well out of my reach."

He looked and sounded sincere. Evan recognized himself in Risk in that moment. He'd felt the same when he'd kissed Bleidd. Like he'd reached for someone too far above him and had been smacked back to reality. Evan found himself closing the distance between them. He captured Risk's mouth once more, kissing him deep and coming up panting when he pulled away. "You're not beneath me. I'm not turning you away. This isn't about that. My first duty is to Baptiste, and I've stayed away too long." Evan held Risk's gaze as he made the claim, ensuring the man saw his honesty. He would get to the bottom of whatever was going on with Bleidd, but—so far— Bleidd was the one who'd shown himself to be underhanded, always tearing Evan away from anyone who might want him. He couldn't trust that Bleidd wasn't pulling the same shit again. Especially in light of the revelations about how he would elevate a mate's stature. Risk was the only man who Evan couldn't find an ulterior motive for wanting him.

Obviously reassured, Risk nodded. "Of course." The scenery around them transformed even as Risk held his stare. The smell of the bayou was replaced with the odor of unwashed bodies and stale liquor. They were behind the Voodoo shop. "You're not like other wolves," Risk said, sounding somewhat confused.

A smile pulled at Evan's lips. "I'll take that as a

compliment," he said before dropping his voice to a conspiratorial whisper. "Don't forget. I got banished."

Risk's expression cleared. A gorgeous smile appeared. "I'll bet they're regretting that now."

"Probably not," Evan admitted with a shake of his head. "But fuck 'em. I'm done living in their no fun zone. Vampires have accepted me in ways Weres never have."

A soft chuckle escaped Risk. The sound had butterflies stirring in Evan's stomach. Risk eyed him for a moment before sighing. "I won't kiss you again tonight," he said, leaving Evan disappointed, before adding, "You're too much of a temptation to me. Another night?"

"Another night," Evan agreed.

"Until then," Risk said, disappearing.

Evan waited for a few minutes, ensuring Risk didn't decide to come back before stripping and transforming. If he stuck to the shadows, he could move faster as a wolf. He couldn't drag Baptiste into this. Baptiste was loyal. If Bleidd was in real trouble, Baptiste might leave him there. Plus, this was a job for the king. If Bleidd wasn't in danger, he would be once Evan got hold of him.

## 5

Dougal's soft blond locks brushed Lire's thighs each time he swallowed Lire's cock. The sensation was making it damn hard for Lire to concentrate on the mate currently straddling his face. The closer he got to the edge, the harder he tried pleasing Faolan. He hallowed out his cheeks, sucking hard even as he pumped two fingers inside the sexy ginger's ass. The headboard made a loud cracking sound beneath Faolan's hold. A roar of triumph ran through Lire. He knew Faol was close. Lire stroked the man's chest and stomach as he quickened his motions. Dougal's throat tightened on Lire's cock. The pressure beating at his crown wouldn't be denied. Everything went quiet. Lire held his breath. Every muscle in his body tensed. An explosion of ecstasy rocked him. Before he could recover, Dougal shifted to his knees and impaled Lire's ass with his cock. Another wave of pleasure overcame him.

In his excitement, Lire went above and beyond to steal Faolan's orgasm. Lire swore even Faolan's roar of satisfaction as he pumped Lire's mouth full of cum had a Scottish accent. Lire swallowed as quickly as he could. Faolan's amethyst gaze watched Lire's every move. Lire made a show of licking Faolan's dick, driven by the giant vampire's lust-filled expression. Dougal pumped at just the right angle, dragging a moan from Lire. Faolan traced Lire's lips with his crown, making Lire hotter by the second. Long, dark strands of hair stuck to Lire's sweat-covered skin. Faolan pushed his hair away as he shifted positions and captured Lire's mouth, licking as if he searched for any hint of his own cum. In all his years of living, which were vast, Lire had never had anyone make him hotter than the mates he'd been blessed with. He would give them anything.

"I love you both so much," Lire whispered between kisses.

Dougal deepened his strokes. The sound of skin slapping mixed with soft moans and the scent of sex. As a lilin demon, Lire was in his version of heaven, drowning in passion. With their minds fully connected, Lire felt Dougal crest. Then, he exploded, and another wave of ecstasy rolled through Lire. His cock jumped, pumping hot cum onto his stomach and chest. Faolan whimpered as he pulled Dougal in to join their kiss. He didn't deserve this happiness. Lire knew it. But he was a demon and had no qualms about taking what he didn't earn.

There was something off tonight. He always recognized he had more than he should, but tonight —even as his men fell asleep in his hold—the feeling of being unworthy wouldn't ease. Once he was certain they wouldn't be disturbed, Lire turned to smoke and shifted from beneath them. He didn't solidify until he was standing outside, surrounded by the night. He closed his eyes and inhaled. The scent of wolf assailed his senses. Lire's eyes shot open, and he searched the source. There was only one wolf who could pass their wards without setting off the alarm. Evan Canagan. Jonathan had given the pup free roam over the property, so he could run in wolf form without fear of being seen.

Lire waved a hand and pants appeared, covering his nudity a half second before Evan padded around the corner. As he ran toward Lire, Evan transformed, becoming a man. He didn't bother hiding his nudity. Wolves weren't known for their modesty. Lire tried not to notice how pretty the boy was, because to him, Evan truly was a boy.

"I need help," Evan said without preamble, bringing Lire's thoughts of beauty to a halt.

"What's happened?"

Evan made a helpless gesture. "I'm not sure, exactly. Look, I know this'll sound crazy, but I was out at Riskel's earlier and I heard Bleidd calling out to me—mentally."

"Okay," Lire said, wondering what he was supposed to think was crazy about that.

"He said Riskel had him pinned with silver chains."

That was getting into the odd category. "Did he say where?"

Evan shook his head. "But I think I have an idea. There's an overgrown path that leads back to old slave quarters. That's where I kept catching his scent." Evan chewed his bottom lip, looking lost and young. "I didn't know where else to go."

Lire fought the urge to pet Evan and ease him. Despite Evan being a guardian wolf, he wasn't a fighter. Maybe he would be someday, but Lire suspected the wolf would never grow out of being sweet. No doubt Odin had a plan for him, but Lire got the feeling the warrior god had done the boy a kindness by bonding him with Baptiste.

"Don't worry," Lire said, calming him. "If Bleidd is being held against his will, I'll find him."

Evan's shoulders fell, as if a weight had been lifted. "Thank you. Do you need some help?"

Oh, he really was sweet. Lire bit back an evil smile. Lire needed his mates to survive, but he needed no one to help him kill. "I've got this. Go home, and I'll keep you posted."

With an agreement in place, Lire watched as Evan transformed back into a wolf and trotted away. Having something productive to do already had Lire feeling better. Evan was Baptiste's wolf. Lire owed Baptiste for life. If he could do this one small thing, maybe he'd be a step closer to deserving the two men currently sleeping in his bed. He just hoped Bleidd Gunnolf was worthy of Evan's concern. For all any of them knew, Riskel had every right to keep the alpha chained.

---

*The boy's thoughts were loud and never ending. It made it impossible to spend much time in his company. Especially since most of Evan's thoughts were about him.*

*The temptation was crippling and so wrong. While Bleidd might have every right to do as he pleased with Evan, he couldn't take advantage.*

*"You're not paying attention, Evan. I've known infants who could concentrate longer."*

*"How old are you?" Evan asked, ignoring Bleidd's lecture. "Because even though your hair is silver, you look closer to twenty-five. Has your hair always been that color?"*

*Bleidd rubbed the spot between his eyes. "I should make you go on a hunt."*

*Evan was already watching a butterfly outside the window and not listening. Bleidd moved closer, poking him in the arm. Evan's gorgeous dark blue gaze swung his way. Bleidd swallowed. The boy should've been hunting from day one, but Bleidd couldn't let Evan mix with the pack. He was special.*

*"You didn't answer my questions."*

*Evan's brain fog was catching. "What?"*

*Evan tapped his head. "Your hair. How old are you?"*

*Bleidd shook his head. "Old enough to know better."*

*"Better than what?"*

*A sigh clogged Bleidd's throat. He tugged Evan from the chair he'd been occupying by the cabin window. "It's time you at least learned a little about being a man.*

First..." Evan stared at his mouth and Bleidd forgot what he planned to say. "What are you—"

Evan's lips touched his. In a flash, Bleidd had two handfuls of Evan's ass, lifting him onto the edge of his desk. Evan's hands were everywhere. Bleidd couldn't stop kneading Evan's body every place he could reach. No one had prepared him for this pup. The moment that thought hit, Bleidd shoved Evan away. This was wrong. Evan hadn't been allowed to live yet. He didn't deserve this. Bleidd would not do this.

"You have to go."

Evan slid from the desk. He looked everywhere but at Bleidd. His pain was stabbing Bleidd through the heart. Bleidd hardened himself against it.

"Okay. I guess I'll see you later."

"No," Bleidd barked, hearing the barely suppressed rage in his voice and incapable of stopping it. "You have to go somewhere else. This clan needs real men. Strong wolves. You're neither."

Evan's expression never changed. "I see."

Bile rose in Bleidd's throat. He'd never hated himself more, and that was saying something. The urge to stroke Evan's jaw and promise to never hurt him was a real thing. He wanted to protect him. Instead, he ripped the man's heart out. "From this moment on, you're banished from the pack."

A sharp pain bit into Bleidd's skin, tearing him from the nightmare of losing Evan the first time. Maybe, if he lived, Bleidd might find the courage to beg Evan's forgiveness. It seemed, every time he tried, he ended up losing his temper instead. No wonder the boy had so easily fallen for Riskel's bullshit. He had to get free. Find Evan. What if Riskel had already done him harm? Silver bit into Bleidd's skin. The more he fought, the deeper the chains dug until he feared he'd lose a limb if he struggled. He'd tried transforming several times without luck. Bleidd had also tried calling out mentally to Eirik. He couldn't reach that far in his weakened state.

Riskel was the king of torture. The vampire could've fed from him or spent hours cutting his skin. Instead, he'd let the silver do its job. It was twenty-four-seven torment. Any loss of blood might have him passing out and missing the fun. Riskel left him to rot and suffer as long as possible. He wondered if bringing Evan close had been a bit of mental torture, or if Bleidd had hallucinated that part. Everything was foggy at this point. The door screeched open. Bleidd expected Riskel had come to finish him off.

"Bleidd." The harsh whisper had Bleidd blinking, trying to clear the haze from his vision.

He tried calling out. Only a croak escaped him. A shadowy figure appeared like smoke. Bleidd squinted, trying to make the person's image solidify. The smoke turned to flesh, revealing a familiar-looking demon.

"Well, shit," Lire said, eyeing Bleidd from head to foot. "I'd hoped Evan was wrong. You're in bad shape. I'll get you to Jonathan, and then we'll come back to take care of Riskel."

Bleidd opened his mouth. Still, no sound emerged. Evan had sent help. He hadn't hallucinated. Lire waved a hand over the chains and they disappeared. With a second wave, Bleidd floated like a feather through space, landing softly upon an unfamiliar bed. Voices that might've been familiar if he wasn't so fucked surrounded him. Cool hands pressed on his wounds, tearing a silent scream from his throat. Jonathan came into view. He glowed like the sun, mesmerizing Bleidd. Then, everything went black.

---

THE SCENT OF MAGIC DIDN'T BRING HIM PEACE.

Nothing did. Evan's skin itched. He held back the wolf inside him by force of will alone as he counted the cash register, getting ready for the day. Three times already, he'd started over when he realized he hadn't been paying attention. Finally, he managed to make it through. With that chore out of the way, Evan unlocked the front door and propped it open. From there, he turned items label out, ensuring everything was straight. Even when Baptiste joined him, Evan didn't stop. He couldn't stand still. If he did, he might burst from his skin.

"Are you ever going to tell me about yesterday?"

At Baptiste's question, Evan stared at him and blinked. For the life of him, he couldn't make the question make sense. "What?"

"Yesterday," Baptiste repeated. "You know, your back-to-back dates."

"Oh."

A large frame coming through the door and blocking out the light pulled Evan's attention its way. Lire's gaze swept the room. Oxygen filled Evan's lungs at an exaggerated rate. He forced his feet to stay still as Lire headed his way. He wanted to rush across the room, meet him halfway, and demand to know everything. It had been the night from hell, waiting for word. He'd opened the shop, trying to stick to his daily routine. In truth, all he wanted was to storm Jonathan's house, imploring someone tell him what happened.

"I've got him," Lire said without preamble, sparing Evan from asking.

His knees weakened. "Thank you for going after him." Evan was afraid to say more. Otherwise, his feelings might pour out.

"He was badly injured. The silver chains had cut through his larynx, stopping him from speaking. Jonathan has healed most his wounds, and he's sleeping it off."

"What?" Baptiste said, elbowing his way in between them. "What's happened?"

Lire's gaze moved between them. His expression gave nothing away. It didn't have to. Evan knew he should've already told Baptiste everything, but his voice wouldn't work. He couldn't admit to being in love with someone who hated him even though he was certain Baptiste already knew that part.

Lire saved him from having to explain. "It seems Riskel has a grievance against Bleidd. Rather than coming to the king, or taking it up with Eirik, he chose to take matters in hand. He had Bleidd locked down in silver chains on his property. Evan heard his cries last night and brought the matter to us."

Baptiste's light green gaze locked on Evan, making him feel like the worst of friends. "You should've come to me. I would've sat up with you. We could've dealt with this together," Baptiste said, running his hand down Evan's arm. He needed Baptiste's touch. It kept him sane.

Evan swallowed. If he hadn't gone to Lire, Bleidd might've died. That was all Evan could deal with at the moment. He met Lire's gaze. "I appreciate the update." His voice sounded hoarse and Evan couldn't control it. "What about Riskel?" Evan asked, trying to stay calm. His chest felt heavy and his eyes burned.

"He's disappeared. Jonathan hasn't figured out how he's hiding from him yet, but he will."

Evan nodded. "Thank you for letting me know."

"We'll keep an eye out for him as well," Baptiste assured him.

Lire gave him a sharp nod. "We appreciate the help." He focused on Evan. "If you'd like to come see him, you're welcome to. Jonathan would love to hear your side of things."

Evan nodded. It was getting harder by the second to pretend he didn't care. "Um, I don't really know much other than what I told you last night. Risk and I went for a walk on his property, and I thought I caught Bleidd's scent, then I heard him call out. Since I wasn't sure of what I'd heard, I thought it best to bring it to Jonathan rather than confronting Risk."

"You did good," Lire said, reaching out as if he meant to pat his arm before immediately pulling away again.

Evan got it. He flashed Lire an understanding smile. "Kallus does that too sometimes. He forgets he shouldn't touch people." Evan shrugged. "It happens."

Lire tilted his head to one side and eyed Evan as if trying to work through a puzzle. Evan got that too. He was odd. Most people were confused by him. "You're incorruptible," Lire said suddenly as if he'd finally found the answer he'd been looking for. "I've never actually come across a soul like yours in all my years." A bright smile stretched the demon's lips, making him look like an angel rather than the demon he was. "You must keep this one," he said, motioning toward Baptiste, "pacing the floor at night, worrying how he'll keep the world from destroying you."

A pain sliced through Evan's chest and he dropped his gaze to hide his wince. Everyone thought he was weak. Thankfully, Baptiste didn't agree. He just kept rubbing Evan's back.

"That was a compliment," Lire said, bringing Evan's gaze back to his. Lire meant it. He was trying to be nice, but Evan didn't understand. "Most people want to be like you," Lire explained. "But life just kicks it out of them." Lire shook his head. "I know I'm explaining myself badly. You're sweet, and you obviously care about others, even when they don't deserve it. Don't let life steal that from you." He leaned closer. "And don't let some arrogant asshole make you feel like you're less because you're good to him when he doesn't deserve it."

Evan fought back a smile. "I feel like I just saw a little bit of my dad in you."

Lire winked. "I'm old. It happens."

Despite everything, Evan's smile won. Lire and his clan would take care of Bleidd. His alpha was in good hands. The pains in his chest would pass. Bleidd had never needed him in the past. Now was no different.

"I should get back," Lire said, flashing him a final smile.

Evan nodded. "Thanks again for keeping me posted."

Lire headed for the door. He looked back. "The

offer still stands. If you want to come and sit with him, we'll keep an eye out for you."

Evan nodded and gave him a small smile. It fell the moment Lire was gone. His gaze slid Baptiste's way. The concern in his eyes made Evan feel like shit. Lately, all he'd done was worry Baptiste with his problems and mood swings.

Without a word of admonishment, Baptiste wrapped Evan in a tight hug. "Go to him. I know you want to." He pulled away and held Evan's stare, ensuring Evan saw the honesty in his eyes. "You don't ever have to worry I'll judge you. In fact," he said, moving to their work station behind the counter and picking up a small container, "take some of the healing salve we made with you and see for yourself he'll be fine. Until you do, you won't feel better," he said, holding out the salve.

Evan crossed the room and accepted the vial. The man was perfect in every way. "I hope Eirik and Kallus know how lucky they are to have you."

"They'd better," Baptiste said with a laugh before turning serious. "Take my SUV and come back when you're ready. Just don't forget to check in so I know you're okay. Otherwise, I'll worry all night."

Without thought, Evan shot forward and kissed Baptiste's cheek. "I love you."

Baptiste grabbed him around the waist before he could get away. He held on, hugging Evan and squeezing out the hurt. "I love you too, baby. Next time, come get me. I'll never let anything bad happened to you, even if that means racing to the rescue of that giant asshole."

Evan's throat swelled. "I know."

He set Evan away. "Now go."

With a nod, Evan headed out back for Baptiste's SUV. He should've gone to Baptiste first. The problem was, he was embarrassed to care about Bleidd. Over and over again, Bleidd broke him. Yet, Evan never walked away. Eventually, no one would support him on that road. Evan wasn't sure even he could take it any longer. He would do this—for himself—and then he was done with Bleidd Gunnolf.

———

SOMETHING SOFT AND WARM STROKED HIS WRIST. Bleidd's eyelids had never felt so heavy. Before he opened his eyes, Bleidd smelled him. His cock stirred. The muscles in his stomach cramped with need. Bleidd was paralyzed with want. Evan leaned across him, stroking Bleidd's other wrist. A warming sensation began in that arm as well. Bleidd tried prying his eyes open to see what was being done, but it was too hard. His lids wouldn't lift. Bleidd swallowed. It hurt. The pain wasn't sharp as it had been. Instead, his throat had become like sandpaper, harsh and irritating. He took another deep breath, inhaling Evan's scent into his lungs. The pup was like wild flowers, innocence, and moonlight all wrapped into one. Bleidd couldn't get enough.

"Evan."

He felt the air shift as Evan's name passed his lips. Evan's fingers went still on Bleidd's wrist. "I'm here."

Need clawed at Bleidd's gut. He'd gone slow. His patience was wearing thin. Evan belonged to him. Bleidd's hand shot out. In one swift motion, he had Evan pulled into the bed with him and tucked beneath him. His lips found Evan's. Evan never hesitated kissing him. Today was no different. The boy gave back as good as he got. Bleidd's hands massaged every place he could reach. Evan felt amazing beneath his palms. Bleidd tore at the boy's clothes, craving his bare skin. Even without his eyesight, he had no trouble getting Evan nude.

Evan whimpered around Bleidd's tongue and kneaded Bleidd's back while writhing beneath him.

This pup wanted him. He was so fucking responsive, begging to get fucked. Inky black jealousy reared its ugly head. Evan was his and only his. Yet he'd been with Riskel last night. Bleidd hadn't imagined that. Evan had let the vampire kiss him. Stroke him. Had he let him do anything else?

Bleidd found himself jacking Evan's hard cock, trying to bring him pleasure even in his rage. His eyelids finally worked. He stared down at the most gorgeous man he'd ever met. Dark blue eyes framed by jet black lashes and made brighter by the flush of Evan's cheeks stared up at him.

Bleidd couldn't stop the accusations. "Did you do this with him? Did he kiss you like this? Touch you like this?" Bleidd punctuated each word with a squeeze.

Evan blinked. His confusion was almost tangible. "Who?"

"Riskel," Bleidd spat while wondering how many men there were to choose from. "Were you beneath him last night while I was trapped beneath his chains?"

The lust died in Evan's face, turning to hate. Bleidd's throat burned and it no longer had anything to do with silver. He had a terrible feeling he'd just killed something beautiful—like ripping the wings from a butterfly.

Evan shoved his way out from beneath him. In a flash, a black wolf leapt over him, landing with a thud on the wooden floor. Bleidd rolled. Evan tried scooping his clothes up in his mouth, obviously intent on leaving in wolf form. Bleidd dove for his back leg, determined to drag him back to bed. Evan twisted, flying into a growling rage of teeth and claws. A cry escaped Bleidd as the skin ripped from his arm as Evan's powerful jaw clamped down. Bleidd jerked his hand away. Blood splashed across the sheets. With one last menacing growl, Evan scooped his clothes into his jaw and burst from the room. Bleidd held his injured arm against his chest and stared at the spot where Evan had been. The ache in his chest was all on him. When it came to Evan, Bleidd was always an idiot. He loved the boy. Always had, and all Bleidd ever did was slap Evan down for daring to make him feel a thing. He was such an old fool.

---

EVAN'S HEART RACED. BLOOD POUNDED IN HIS EARS. The tangy flavor of iron coated his tongue. Jonathan had tried stopping him, but Evan didn't stop running until he was safely inside Baptiste's SUV once more. He tried catching his breath while pulling on his clothes. Fucking Bleidd. Evan had let the alpha screw with his head again. No one made him feel so cheap and unwanted. There was zero excuse for Evan continuing to do this to himself. He had no one else to blame.

Once he was dressed, Evan scrubbed at his face before dropping his forehead to the steering wheel. He was such a fucking moron. Evan needed something. Anything. The way Bleidd made him feel was choking the life from him. All the undeserved accusations pumped through his veins, fueling his insanity and fury. With no plan in mind, Evan drove. Trees passed. Nothing registered but Bleidd's voice in his head. Years of rejection and scathing insults weighed on his shoulders. He needed to feel wanted. For any reason.

Evan blinked at Saber's cabin, wondering how he'd gotten there and how he hadn't killed anyone along the way. The SUV had driven itself. Evan's pain refused to let another emotion in. He'd been reaching for someone who didn't want him for so long he was broken. Even Evan didn't know why he'd never let anyone make love to him. It was like, since the first time he'd set eyes on Bleidd, no one else had measured up. That stopped today. He was tired of being unwanted. Neglected.

Evan's feet carried him to the door. He didn't let himself think. This was for the best. It didn't matter if Saber was after some payout Evan hadn't known existed. At least, he pretended to want Evan. That was more than anyone else ever did. Riskel didn't count since he was obviously crazy. Right now, Evan just needed someone to fuck him and make him feel something other than worthless. Everything hurt.

Each breath Evan took came harder than the last as his knuckles connected with the wood. He no longer cared what happened to him. It didn't matter. No one would ever love him. He wasn't even sure if he loved himself anymore. The door swung open and a blonde woman stared out at him. She looked slightly familiar, but Evan couldn't place where he'd seen her. Her gaze dropped to Evan's feet before slowly lifting back to meet his gaze. Her smile made him feel like he'd just been molested.

"Are you here to join the fun? Please say yes."

"Um," Evan said, shifting uncomfortably. "Is Saber around?"

She glanced behind her, accidentally letting the door slip open enough for Evan to spot Saber between another blonde's thighs. He turned his face away. His stomach churned. Nothing was right any longer. Everyone was fake. He couldn't take the pain. Everything was too much.

"He's busy with my sister right now," the woman said with a giggle. "Would you like to join us?"

Evan couldn't even try for a smile. Agony owned him in every way. "No, thank you. Have a great night." Without waiting for her response, Evan turned to go.

"Whoa. Wait up, Evan," Saber called at his back.

Evan swallowed down his hurt. He shoved his hands in his pockets to hide the way they shook before he turned back and focused on Saber. His jeans were on, but they weren't zipped or buttoned. Every other inch of Saber was nude, showing the scratches marring his skin. Evan thought to blow off the situation, but his throat wasn't having it. He was too far gone.

Saber looked worried. "I wasn't expecting you. Is everything okay?"

"Yeah." No one was more surprised than Evan by how steady he sounded. "Sorry. I should've called first or whatever."

For a full minute, they simply stared at each other. There was nothing to say. Evan's throat swelled to the point he could barely breathe. There was no one or nothing for him here or anywhere.

Saber motioned toward the house. "Let me get rid of everyone and we can talk."

A bitter smile pulled at Evan's lips. "No. That's not... I mean, I guess I already knew..." Evan blew out a breath. With a shake of his head, Evan walked away. Lire's lecture came back to haunt him. He saw it now. Life did kick the kindness from people. People always wrecked him because he was nice. As he climbed inside Baptiste's SUV and backed down the drive, Evan purposely didn't look Saber's way again. His heart couldn't take another thing tonight. He'd said it before, but this time it was true. Evan was done. With everything.

## 6

Bleidd paced the bedroom he'd been assigned. Since Evan ran out, the room felt more like a prison. As much as he wanted to hunt down Evan, the king had other plans for him. With Riskel still on the loose, they wanted Bleidd where they could watch him. He understood. They'd already had to save him once, and he still wasn't one hundred percent. Once he was healed, he'd have more choices. Bleidd ran his hands through his hair and scrubbed. Fuck. Everything was a mess. Why did he always lash out at Evan? Some people thought age brought cleverness. In Bleidd's case, that wasn't true. Age had given him anger issues.

His bedroom door opened, and Baptiste stepped inside. The Druid looked furious. Eirik was on the man's heels, looking ready to snag his man around the waist if he pounced. "You're coming with me," Baptiste said before Bleidd had time to bow.

Bleidd's gaze moved between the two. "I thought Jonathan wanted me to stay here."

Eirik looked panicked as he made a slashing motion across his throat behind Baptiste, and Bleidd quickly added, "But, of course, I'm at your service."

"I know you are," Baptiste snapped. "But first, let's get a couple of things straight," Baptiste said, not sounding anywhere near appeased by Bleidd's agreement. "I hate your face and you're a piece of shit."

"Okay," Bleidd said, dragging out the word, sounding every bit as confused as he felt.

Baptiste talked over the top of him. "You broke my wolf and you will fix him or I will break you."

Bleidd blinked. "What's wrong with Evan?"

"You," Baptiste growled, pointing at Bleidd. "You're what's wrong with him. I sent him over here yesterday to be with you, and he comes in late last night in wolf form, refusing to change back or talk to anyone. I don't know what you did, but you will fucking fix it."

Goddamn it. Bleidd rubbed his chest. He'd known he'd upset Evan, but he'd never suspected Evan would let it bring him down. Evan had never let Bleidd destroy him before now. "Let's go," Bleidd said, moving close to Baptiste despite the man's open hostility. Evan needed him.

Baptiste nodded, as if satisfied by Bleidd's reaction. That didn't mean the man was gentle when he grabbed Bleidd's arm and pulled him through space to an unfamiliar hallway. Baptiste knocked on a closed door. "Evan, I'm coming in." Baptiste opened the door as he made the claim. Bleidd was on his heels.

Bleidd moved around Baptiste at the first sight of Evan. As Baptiste claimed, he was in wolf form. Of course, Bleidd wouldn't have known it except for the two black scruffy ears poking out between where the pillow covered his face and the blanket covered his body on the bed. Bleidd didn't wait for permission. He crossed the room and sat on the edge of the bed.

"Are you all right, Evan?" Bleidd asked, moving the pillow away.

Evan turned his face away.

"Is all this because of yesterday?"

Evan didn't move. Not even an ear twitch.

Bleidd tried skimming Evan's thoughts. Nothing. All Bleidd got from Evan was a choking sadness.

"I didn't mean it," Bleidd said quietly.

Baptiste exploded. "You motherfucker. I knew it. I knew this was all your fault."

Eirik lifted the man from the floor before he could attack. "Okay. That's enough of that, baby. Let's leave them to it," Eirik said, trying to soothe Baptiste as he hauled the man from the room.

The moment they were gone, Bleidd crossed the room and shut the door. He turned the lock. "For Odin to bless someone with a wolf companion, he must first recognize them as a warrior," Bleidd said as he moved back to the bed. He took off his shirt. "I must confess, before this moment, I never believed the rumors about Baptiste killing a house full of demons. Now I'm thinking I'll never sleep with both eyes closed again," he added with a chuckle. Evan didn't react. Not to his words or to him stripping.

Bleidd transformed. He pawed the edge of the bed, wondering if the frame would support their combined weight. In this form, he was a lot bigger. When the mattress didn't protest, Bleidd leapt onto the bed. Without preamble, he straddled Evan's body and dropped full weight on top of him, squishing him to the mattress.

Evan immediately became human again, gasping and sputtering for air. Bleidd had him trapped facedown. "What the hell?"

Bleidd changed back. He recognized his mistake the moment their nude skin melded. His lips found Evan's nape without thought. "It lives," he whispered against the man's skin. Chill bumps rose beneath his lips. Bleidd's cock stirred. He didn't try hiding it. His lips moved to the spot beneath Evan's ear. "You can be mad all you want, but don't shut me out. Tell me you hate me. Call me a bastard."

"I can't breathe," Evan said, sounding disconnected.

"If you can talk, you can breathe." Oddly, Bleidd was having fun. He hadn't felt so light in years.

"For fuck's sake. If I let you fuck me, will you go away?"

Bleidd swallowed down a laugh. "Way to kill the mood."

"The dick poking me would suggest otherwise."

Bleidd lifted just enough to stare down the line of his body at his erection. His lust skyrocketed at the sight of his cock on Evan's beautiful body. "I don't know what you're talking about," Bleidd said, settling back down.

Evan growled. It was hot. "You don't want me. Not really, so why are you doing this? Is it the money? I'll pay you to go away."

Confusion had Bleidd trying to see Evan's

expression. He had no clue what Evan meant. "What money?"

Evan tapped the mattress, showing his aggravation. "I'm a guardian wolf," Evan said, as if it should clear up everything. When he didn't respond right away, Evan sighed. "Whoever I choose as my mate gets a god's dowry."

Evan's explanation cleared up nothing. "Who told you that?"

"Does it matter?" Evan asked, sounding tired.

"Yes, because it's not true."

Evan glanced over his shoulder. "Then why is everyone chasing after me and fucking up my life?"

Bleidd rolled to his side, freeing Evan. He faced Evan and held his stare. "Everyone is chasing you because you're young and gorgeous. Anyone would be blessed to have you. Everyone is fucking up your life because we're stupid assholes who don't deserve you. I just wanted you to have time to enjoy life, Evan. You can't begin to fathom how long forever is, and I don't want you to regret choosing me."

"I haven't chosen you," Evan said, getting some fire back in his eyes. "You're mean, and you don't like me. Everything I do annoys you. You don't think anyone should enjoy life. Everything is duty and being a real man. Plus, you don't like to kiss. I love kissing," Evan said with a sniff.

The sound made Bleidd smile. "Well, baby, if that's how you feel, I'm about to crush your heart. I'm your fated mate."

Evan blinked. "What?"

"You can hear my thoughts and I can hear yours," Bleidd explained. "Only mates can do that."

Evan sat up. Bleidd damn near swallowed his tongue at the full show of Evan's body. "That can't be true. I can hear Baptiste and Eirik."

"Eirik is our god and Baptiste is your person. And, I'm your wolf." Bleidd flashed him a sad smile. "Sorry you didn't get someone younger and better looking."

Evan stared at him in silence for so long, Bleidd wondered if he'd checked out. "My parents used to have all these conversations mentally. It was maddening because they were usually talking about me. Or inappropriately, which was equally horrifying." It was obvious by the way Evan kept swallowing, it hurt him to talk about his parents, so Bleidd stayed quiet. Evan dropped his gaze to his hands. "I'm sorry you got stuck with me. If you want to live on opposite sides of the planet and never see each other, then that's what we'll do."

Bleidd's heart couldn't take it. He toyed with Evan's fingers. "That's not what I want." Evan's gaze moved his way, as if hanging on his every word. A smile tugged at Bleidd's lips. "When you came to me at seventeen, I was horrified to hear the nonstop chatter going on inside your head. I knew right away you were mine, but you were *seventeen*." Even Bleidd heard the horror in his voice. "Then, you kissed me. I'd never been so immediately consumed by anyone. I knew right away you didn't kiss me out of lust. You kissed me because you felt so strongly about me that words were no longer enough. Actions were all that was left to you. You have no idea how overcome I was by that. But you weren't ready for me, and I couldn't trust myself. I sent you away." Bleidd took a breath. "It was like ripping my heart out and tossing it away. Your face." He swallowed. Bleidd could still see Evan's pain-filled gaze as he'd sent him away. He brought Evan's hand to his mouth. "I just didn't want you to be unhappy with me," Bleidd said against his skin. "I've lived so long. You've not had that chance." Evan was here, and the pup was no worldlier than when Bleidd sent him away four years earlier. But he realized something now he hadn't then—Evan would never be worldly. He possessed an innocence that couldn't be tainted and Bleidd wanted to protect it. Bleidd needed to know someone like Evan existed. He made the world seem less corrupt.

Evan gently tugged his hand away. "My place is with Baptiste now."

Bleidd sat up. "I know, and my place is with you. Wherever you are," he added, touching Evan's cheek. He inched closer. "I have another confession," he whispered, hoping he wouldn't spook Evan. "I fucking love kissing you," he said, capturing Evan's lips. With a tug, he tumbled backward, taking Evan with him without breaking their kiss. Evan's body covered his. Bleidd loved the way Evan's body felt against him. Having Evan sprawled across his chest and straddling his hips was pure heaven. Possessiveness roared through him. The need to claim his mate was stronger than anything Bleidd ever experienced before. He couldn't stop himself from rolling and pinning Evan beneath him. His hips moved of their own volition. He craved the sensation of Evan on his dick. His teeth itched to tear into Evan's skin, holding him in place as he claimed the man as his mate for eternity.

Bleidd squeezed his eyes shut and pressed his forehead to Evan's chest, fighting his nature. "I don't know if I can be gentle."

Evan stroked his hair. "It's okay."

Evan sounded so damn sure that Bleidd was turning him away again that Bleidd's head shot up. He needed Evan to see the lust in his eyes. Evan wouldn't escape him unscathed this time, but he needed the man to understand. "If we do this, you're mine."

Evan's traced Bleidd's jawline with his fingertips. "From what you've said, that's already true. I feel it tugging at my chest," Evan added in a whisper, as if he thought Bleidd might think his confession was ridiculous.

Bleidd couldn't have that. Everything Evan felt was how it should be. They'd been paired long before either of them had been created. "It's here," Bleidd said, tapping his sternum. "Like an invisible string is luring me closer to you, and I'll go insane if I don't follow, but I don't want you to feel tricked. The moment I claim you, you've lost your chance to escape. You'll be mine and I'll be yours. Being apart will be physically painful and no one else will ever be enough. If you don't want me, say so now. I'll never let you go if you let me in."

"I want you."

Damn. The stunning purity Evan bled dripped from each word, leaving Bleidd breathless in awe of the man's quiet strength. Evan's power was in his unshakable trust and loyalty. He possessed the most beautiful soul Bleidd had ever seen.

"I don't want to hurt you."

"You won't," Evan said. His trust humbled Bleidd. The way he stared at Bleidd had Bleidd willing to do anything and every damn thing to ensure Evan only experienced pleasure. Bleidd couldn't let Evan go into this blind.

"I'll bite you. You're my mate. I won't be able to stop myself from marking you as mine."

To his surprise, a bright smile stretched Evan's lips. "That's only fair, since I bit you yesterday."

Bleidd held up his arm. "I'm good. See? All healed."

Evan's gaze swept over Bleidd's arm before his fingertips followed suit. "It scarred."

Bleidd's mouth lifted in one corner. "That's because it's you. You're the only one capable of marking me. Just as I'm the only one capable of marking you." If Evan was any other wolf, Bleidd would be amazed by how much the boy didn't know about their kind, but Evan came from a small pack in Greenland that had been wiped out by Mammon when Evan was younger. It only took a moment in Evan's company to want to keep him from corruption. No doubt his family had fed the pup's innocence.

Evan's gaze met his. There was nothing innocent about Evan in that moment. Unadulterated hunger stared at Bleidd. Bleidd could barely breathe in the face of so much open desire.

"Anyone who sees this will know you're mated. That you're mine."

Bleidd had to take a breath. Evan sounded so damn possessive. It was everything he wanted. "Yes. Just as everyone will see your marks and know you're mine." The hard cock leaking between them spoke volumes about how much Evan wanted the picture Bleidd painted.

"I want to taste you. Will you let me?"

Bleidd wondered if this boy would cripple him with his guileless seduction, but he didn't want to make any assumptions. "How do you mean?"

Evan pushed, urging Bleidd onto his back. "Like this," he said, dipping his head and opening his mouth over a spot on Bleidd's chest. *Always wanted this.* Bleidd's eyes fell closed as Evan's thoughts washed over him.

*Watch it, pup. Your thoughts will have this show ending before I'm ready.*

Evan's soft chuckle vibrated against Bleidd's skin

as he kissed a path down Bleidd's body. "I would keep your secret," Evan said before circling Bleidd's navel with his tongue while managing to also lightly lick Bleidd's crown.

A hiss escaped Bleidd. He already knew he wouldn't let Evan be in control for long. Evan was too tempting.

Evan brushed his lips across Bleidd's crown in the lightest of kisses. A blaze roared to life inside Bleidd, nearly doubling him over in desire. His skin itched. The wolf inside threatened to burst out. Bleidd ground his back teeth. He didn't want to discourage Evan from exploring his body. Evan's tongue shot out, swiping away his pre-cum.

*Mhmm.*

Bleidd exploded into action. His patience gone. In a flash, he had Evan facedown, one hand wrapped around the man's throat, keeping him from getting away.

*There's lube in the drawer.*

Bleidd's gaze shot to the bedside table. Everything had a red haze coating it. He dove for the drawer, finding the bottle Evan promised would be there. With the oil coating his fingers, Bleidd toyed with Evan's asshole. *We'll discuss later why you have this.*

Evan writhed against him, pushing closer and silently begging for more. Bleidd positioned his cock at Evan's asshole. Air rushed into his lungs as his chest heaved.

*Please?*

Bleidd couldn't take Evan begging. He tried moving slow. He didn't want to hurt him. The beast inside him wasn't having it. He kept going until he was buried root deep. The madness didn't subside. The tugging in his chest he'd described earlier became a forceful drag, yanking him closer to the edge of the unknown. All Bleidd knew was he'd never be the same after this. He could feel everything Evan felt. Bleidd had never been more connected with anyone. It was addictive. He was high with pleasure. Bleidd pulled back, slowly pumping. He couldn't hurt this man. This one was his mate.

"Don't stop."

At Evan's plea, Bleidd lowered his weight onto one elbow and buried his hand between Evan and the mattress, palming Evan's erection. He pumped in time with his cock sawing in and out of Evan's ass. Damn. He was so tight and hot. Sweat covered Bleidd's brow. His gums itched as his teeth grew. He couldn't hold back the wolf. The tiny mewling noises

Evan made had Bleidd ready to pound him—hard. Evan wasn't ready for that. The beast inside him didn't care.

*Evan, I can't control myself. I can't contain the wolf.*

Evan pushed against him, taking his pleasure. Bleidd could feel how close he was to explosion. "Fuck me," Evan growled, sounding every bit as desperate as Bleidd felt.

Bleidd snapped. Without thought, his teeth tore at Evan's shoulder, sinking into his skin, clamping down and hanging on as he slammed inside him. Blood pooled in his mouth. Evan's moans filled his ears. Evan tensed. Ecstasy burst through him as Evan's orgasm hit, forcing Bleidd over the edge into an abyss of soul-rocking pleasure. Light and sound were lost to him. All Bleidd knew was the man beneath him. Their souls touched and merged, becoming one. Nothing in his life compared to the moment. He licked the bite marks that were already healing, leaving behind scars that marked him as mated. They were beautiful. Bleidd wished the world could see Evan's scars. He needed everyone to know this man belonged to him, so they would understand—if they trespassed—he would tear them limb from limb.

With the immediate desperation passing, Bleidd

could focus again. Evan's thoughts were all over the place. Bleidd couldn't pin down his mood. They were a mess of sweat and cum. Bleidd had no desire to move. He held Evan tighter, hugging him to his chest. His lips brushed Evan's scars. He couldn't stop. His emotions swelled. Evan was being too quiet. A shot of fear ran through Bleidd.

Bleidd rolled to his side, freeing Evan. "Did I hurt you?" Even Bleidd heard the panic in his voice.

Evan turned his head, meeting Bleidd's stare. His face was flushed, and his eyes were red-rimmed. Bleidd's panic doubled. Then, Evan opened his mouth and wrecked Bleidd. "I'm not alone anymore." His voice was hoarse and broken.

Bleidd's eyes burned. For the first time, he recognized the truth. In the past four years, he hadn't given Evan his freedom and a chance to love. He'd made him an outcast with no family until Odin had bonded him with Baptiste. Even then, Baptiste was a vampire. There was still that missing piece from Evan's life—other wolves. He'd been alone. Because he couldn't take it back, Bleidd kissed Evan, pouring his heart into the moment.

"I'm sorry I ever hurt you," he said between kisses. Bleidd swiped Evan's hair back from his face and spent several minutes switching between sucking the man's bottom lip and placing light kisses in the corner of Evan's mouth. There were too many thoughts in his head and emotions in his chest. Evan deserved a better mate, but Bleidd was who he'd gotten. Bleidd brushed his lips over Evan's mouth. "I know I have no right to ask, but I need something from you."

Evan pulled away. His gaze moved over Bleidd's face. "Anything."

Bleidd never stopped being blown away by Evan's giving nature. "Let me hold you," Bleidd begged. "Just stay here with me. Be still and let me hang on to the mate I never thought to have."

A sweet smile touched Evan's lips as he snuggled close. "I'll try to be still," he promised as Bleidd's arms locked around him. "You know how busy my mind is."

"Let your mind run free, baby," Bleidd said, kissing him on the head. "I love listening to your nonstop internal chatter. It's soothing."

"Wow," Evan breathed against his chest. "Now I know you were meant for me. I drive everyone else crazy."

Evan drove Bleidd crazy too. Just in a different way. It made him insane the way he craved every second of Evan's time. He thought madness would engulf him every time he thought about never seeing Evan again. Bleidd was certain he'd completely crack if Evan never loved him. Evan didn't know the definition of crazy. Bleidd had been there since the first moment he set eyes on Evan and realized he was lost.

## 7

E ven the sunshine looked brighter than usual. Bleidd had been gone when Evan finally woke, but Evan didn't sweat it. He could feel his mate's presence nearby. Evan showered, ate breakfast, and opened the shop. The whole time, his brain stayed locked on Bleidd. His mate was doing something with Eirik. He could hear Bleidd's thoughts. They were all business and boring. Evan tuned out the words and focused on the cadence. Bleidd was a peaceful presence in the back on his mind at all times, soothing Evan.

Baptiste appeared from nowhere and placed a loud kiss on Evan's cheek, pulling a chuckle from him. "There's my gorgeous wolf. You have the perfect I'm-now-mated glow about you."

Heat rushed to Evan's cheeks. "Shut up."

A loud bark of laughter filled the shop. "You should be used to me knowing everything by now." Baptiste's face cleared. He looked more serious than Evan had seen him in a while. "I just want you to be happy. You have no idea how much I love you and want you to smile."

Evan's eyes burned. He loved Baptiste. The vampire was his family. Without Baptiste, Evan didn't know where he would've ended up. He had to clear his throat to speak. "Thank you for being my vampire." Even to Evan's ears, he sounded hoarse.

Baptiste opened his mouth to respond. The sound of a motorcycle drew Evan's gaze to the window. Saber pulled up outside.

"Shit," Evan said, diving down an aisle in hopes that Saber didn't spot him.

A line appeared between Baptiste's brows. "What?"

"It's Saber," Evan explained in a stage whisper, even though there was no way the tiger could hear him.

Baptiste glanced toward the door and shrugged. "So. Just tell him you're mated now and to fuck off."

"You don't understand," Evan said, still whispering, because he couldn't stop. "The last time I saw him, I caught him fucking some girl."

Baptiste's eyebrows rose. "While he was pursuing you?"

Evan nodded. "I guess I don't have much right to be upset. It's not like I was turning down any dates, but I can't lie, it stung. It happened at the worst possible moment, and—"

"Oh, hell no," Baptiste said, cutting him off and looking deadly. "No one hurts my baby."

A bad feeling overcame Evan. He rushed to fix things. "It's okay. I just don't want to see him again."

"Fuck that," Baptiste growled, staring at Saber through the window with open malice. He waved a hand toward Evan. "*Sed totum occultatum a me manere.* He won't hear or see you."

Evan could feel the magic on his skin. "What are you going to do?"

Baptiste didn't answer. Instead, he moved to stand behind the counter and pasted on a fake smile as Saber strolled through the door, looking exactly like a man who wrecked hearts. "Saber. What brings you in today?"

Saber cast a glance around the shop—like he smelled Evan but couldn't find him. "I'm looking for Evan. Is he around?"

Baptiste leaned over the counter. His face screwed up in confusion. "I'm sorry. What?" He toyed with his ear. "A cauldron blew this morning, and I'm having trouble hearing. You'll have to come closer."

A flash of annoyance crossed Saber's features, making Evan wonder why he hadn't noticed earlier that Saber was an ass. He moved closer to Baptiste. "I said—" Saber jumped back in surprise when Baptiste squirted his face with window cleaner. "What the fuck?" Saber roared, swiping at his face. "What was that?"

"Impotence potion," Baptiste said, tearing a bark of laughter from Evan. "Come back when you're ready to crawl across broken glass, apologizing to my wolf for being a no-good fuck face, and I might give you the cure."

Saber looked panicked. "This is a joke, right? You have to be kidding me. Let me see that," he said, scrambling to grab the bottle.

Baptiste pulled the container back out of his reach and snagged Saber by the throat, dragging him halfway over the counter until they were nose to nose. Vampires were a hundred times stronger than men and fifty times stronger than Weres. Saber didn't stand a chance. Not to mention, Baptiste was blood mated to Saber's ruler. If he touched Baptiste, he was dead.

Baptiste bared his fangs. "If you ever come near my wolf again while not scraping and bowing at his feet, you won't have a dick to worry over being limp. Do you feel me?"

Saber gave as much of a nod as he could while getting zero oxygen. Baptiste shoved him away, sending the tiger scrambling. He didn't look back.

"Holy shit," Evan whispered. Baptiste was the most badass vampire on the planet. The funniest part about it was Baptiste didn't even realize it. He simply took care of his own without thought for his safety.

Baptiste snapped his fingers, and the tingling disappeared from his skin. "There. I don't think you'll have to worry about hiding from him."

Evan stared at Baptiste, speechless. A snort escaped him. Baptiste smiled. Evan's snort turned into a roar of laughter. He tried talking through the burbles in his throat. "You squirted him with glass cleaner. His face. Priceless."

A chuckle fell from Baptiste lips before the man doubled over in laughter.

Evan swiped at his eyes. Happiness grew like he hadn't experienced in years. "I love you."

Baptiste tried calling his laughter under control. "I love you too, sweetie." He turned serious. "I swore

I would never let anyone hurt you. You should know by now that's the truth. Next time you have a problem, promise me you'll talk to me instead of turning wolf and refusing to let me in."

"You have my word," Evan swore.

"What's going on in here?" Eirik asked, coming through the back door with Kallus and Bleidd on his heels.

"Just doing some cleaning," Baptiste said, smiling brightly for his men.

Evan didn't have eyes for anyone other than his silver wolf. The way Bleidd's amber eyes brightened as they landed on Evan had Evan's heart turning over in his chest. He was the reason Bleidd looked happy. That was the most empowering knowledge in the world. Evan forgot about the other three men in the room the moment Bleidd crossed the room and touched him. Bleidd's fingers grazed Evan's jaw before tightening and pulling him forward for a kiss. The backs of Evan's eyes burned as their lips met. Everything in his life had been so damn hard. For the first time, he knew he'd never be alone again. While he'd known he'd always have Baptiste, it wasn't the same as having a mate. His heart turned over in his chest. Bleidd tasted like heaven.

Bleidd was the first to pull away. He bumped noses with Evan and smiled. "Promise to miss me."

Evan eyed him. "Always. Where are you going?"

"We haven't heard from Jonathan about Riskel," Eirik said, answering for Bleidd. "Even though Riskel is a vampire, he hurt one of mine, so I intend to take care of things. Baptiste will stay here with you. Don't worry," Eirik said with a wink. "I'll keep your wolf safe."

Evan's gaze moved back to Bleidd. There was a small part of him that feared for Bleidd's safety. After all, he'd almost died only days earlier. But Bleidd was the strongest wolf Evan knew. He believed in him. "Keep your thoughts open to me," Evan said. He smiled to take the bite out of his demand.

Bleidd captured his lips once more, scattering Evan's thoughts. "Always," he said, sounding breathless when he pulled away. He strolled toward the door. Evan's eyes ate up the way Bleidd's body moved. *You'll have me hard all day if you keep thinking things like that.*

Evan couldn't even work up a blush. *Good.*

Bleidd glanced over his shoulder before clearing the door. The heat in the alpha's eyes had Evan biting back a sigh. He was stupid in love with the hard-headed wolf. Before he could chase after his mate and make a fool of himself, Baptiste pulled Evan's attention his way.

"I think you need something to occupy your mind. Otherwise, you'll worry all day. Give me a few and I'll grab the supplies we need to make a truth serum. That'll give you something else to focus on."

Evan nodded. He couldn't argue with Baptiste's logic. "Sure. Sounds fun. We can use it on Dante and find out if he has any pirate's loot hidden away."

Baptiste's laughter followed him out the back door. The bell above the front door jingled. Evan moved to the end of the aisle, intent on greeting their first customer of the day. No one was there, but the air smelled different. The scent was a familiar one, but Evan couldn't place it.

"Hello?" He didn't care if he looked crazy. Someone was there. He knew it even if he couldn't see them. A whisper floated through the air. Evan couldn't make out the words. A wave of exhaustion washed over him. Then, there was nothing.

---

JONATHAN FOCUSED ON THE BLUEPRINTS SPREAD across Niall's desk. He wanted to add on to their house as quickly as possible, fortifying their security while making room for more people. It was all because he'd had a dream. At first, he'd kept quiet, thinking it was a nightmare like any other, but it kept coming until he'd shared his vision with Niall. Now they were acting. Things would change soon. Evil was coming. He'd have to keep his friends close and their enemies out. His attention was split in too many directions. He'd promised Bleidd he would hunt down Riskel. Right now, Riskel seemed like the least of their worries. Niall made it damn hard for Jonathan to concentrate on anything. He kept swiping kisses across the back of Jonathan's neck as he paced at Jonathan's back.

Finally, Jonathan broke. "Are you bored?"

As if waiting for Jonathan's question, Niall pounced. His palms slid across Jonathan's hips. His erection pressed between their bodies, letting Jonathan know exactly what Niall had on his mind. "Nay, not bored. You're viciously tempting me by wearing my family's plaid today." He inched Jonathan's kilt upward. "And nothing else."

It was true. Even though his Nephilim side kept trying to burst free today, that wasn't the real reason he'd chosen the kilt. It was the way his mates, Niall and Cin, looked at him when he wore their plaid that had him teasing them with it today.

Niall leaned into him, molding to his skin. "I could bend you over right now and fook you. Would you like that?" Niall asked against his ear.

Jonathan's breath left him. "Yes. Do it."

The air stirred behind them. "My king," Lire said, interrupting them.

Jonathan spun, ready to snap over the intrusion. Lire stood side by side with Dougal. In Dougal's arms was a bloody and unconscious Riskel. "What's happened?" He'd ordered the vampire found, not beaten.

Dougal shook his head. "I found him at the edge of the property while making my rounds. He woke for only a few short moments, but he has quite the story to tell."

Jonathan crossed the room and touched Risk's forehead. Everything the man knew Jonathan now did too. Horror overcame him. "Find him a room. We have to find Bleidd."

---

SOMETHING LIGHTLY STROKED HIS CHEEK. HIS LIDS felt heavy. As they lifted, Evan fully expected to find himself in bed with Bleidd, his mate beside him. Instead, Evan found himself staring into a familiar set of whiskey-colored eyes. He blinked. Risk's face became clearer.

"Risk?" Evan's gaze shot around the room. He tried scrambling away from Riskel's touch. Evan couldn't move. His hands screamed in protest. Rope bit into his skin. He squeezed his eyes shut, blinking hard while hoping the scenery changed. It didn't help.

"You're so beautiful."

*Bleidd? Baptiste?* Evan mentally tried reaching anyone to help explain his current circumstances. One minute, he'd been straightening shelves. The next, he was here. Wherever here was.

Risk stroked Evan's face again. "So sweet."

*Oh my god, Evan. Where are you?*

Evan almost cried out in relief as Bleidd's voice brushed his mind. *I don't know.* He tried checking out his surroundings without giving himself away. *Nothing looks familiar. It smells like the swamp mixed with Baptiste's shop.*

"Damn. That scent of innocence is gone."

*What do you mean mixed with Baptiste's shop?*

Evan turned his face away, trying to keep Risk from realizing he was mentally connected with Bleidd.

Risk didn't let up. "Did he hurt you?"

Evan didn't respond.

"Do I have a second reason to kill him?"

*I smell magic.*

"A second reason?" Evan asked, hoping to keep Risk talking. "Where am I? What's going on?"

*Magic? That's good. That's something Baptiste can trace. Stay safe. Don't antagonize him.*

Risk straddled his lap, invading his space. He toyed with the ends of Evan's hair. Evan was scared to move. "You're not alone, you know? Bleidd has always been a judgmental, pretentious ass. You're not the first boy he turned out, leaving them homeless, and an outcast. He hates anyone the least bit different." Risk leaned in and sniffed Evan's neck. "You have a special soul. I smelled it right away. No doubt, Bleidd hates you for that. For being different." Risk dragged his hand down Evan's chest, heading south. "I would appreciate you. Keep you moaning my name."

*Hurry. Please?* Evan didn't want to panic, but he didn't like the direction things were headed. "Why am I bound?" Evan had to keep Risk distracted.

Risk's gaze moved from what his hand was doing back to Evan's face. Lust swam in Risk's eyes. His fangs peeked out from behind the man's slightly parted lips and his eyes looked feverish. There was no missing how turned on Risk was. "I'm keeping you safe. Bleidd will come for you. I won't let him take you."

"I'm confused." Evan might've been trying to keep Risk talking, but he really was completely lost. Risk's actions made no sense.

"You're beautiful," Risk said again, refusing to enlighten Evan.

Evan tried once more to free his hands without luck. "I don't like being tied up." Although Evan sounded calm. He wasn't. Not at all. At his heart, he was a wild animal. He was meant to be free.

Risk's expression turned wicked. "I could make you like it. With me, you'll only know pleasure."

"I'm a wolf. Being restrained goes against my nature." Evan measured every word, doing his best not to incite someone who was obviously crazy. "I don't like being bound."

While stroking Evan's chest, Risk's gaze moved over Evan's face, as if searching for any signs of trickery. Finally, he nodded. "You're right. Keeping you chained is cruel. You've already spent years trapped in the city. It's not my intention to break your spirit." He moved from Evan's lap. "I'm not brutal like Bleidd."

"What did Bleidd do to you?"

"I've already told you," Risk snapped as he circled behind Evan. Evan tensed. Risk took an audible breath. When he spoke again, he sounded like he was biting back his temper. "Bleidd is an elitist. You of all people should understand what it's like to be on the receiving end of prejudice. Only pure-blooded Weres make the cut. The rest are left to either starve or make deals with monsters to survive."

*What did you do to this guy?* Evan had to know. Felt it in his gut. If he planned to stay alive, he needed information.

*That's not Riskel.* Evan blinked at Bleidd's pronouncement.

Evan glanced over his shoulder at the vampire at his back as he untied Evan's hands. *He looks like Risk to me.*

"Aren't all Weres pure-blooded?" Evan asked to keep Risk talking.

Risk's expression transformed from irritated to amused, as if he found Evan's ignorance adorable. He stroked Evan's face. "You are so sweet and sheltered. Odin knew what he was about when he placed you with Baptiste. Just as Baptiste has kept you separate from all the ugly in the world, I will too." He went back to working on the ropes around

Evan's wrists, obviously having no intention of telling Evan what the fuck was going on.

*He looks and sounds like Risk. I can see nor smell any difference.*

Even Bleidd's thoughts sounded winded when he responded, as if running a long distance. *That is Tamil. He is a shape shifter. Well, half shape shifter and half mage. He was brought to me as a child, just as you were. When he proved to be too much, hurting young pups and many other unacceptable things, I banished him. He did not take it well. For years, he's plagued me with mischief. Now that I have a mate, he's found a way to cut me as deeply as he feels I've done to him. I won't let that happen. Keep him talking.*

"What do you plan to do about Bleidd?" Evan asked, following Bleidd's instructions.

Blood rushed back to Evan's fingers as the ropes fell away. "Don't worry over that," Tamil said, leaning in until he was nose to nose with Evan. "You will never have to fear displeasing him again. With me, you'll always come first." A lecherous smile touched the shifter's lips. "I know exactly how to treat sweet boys."

*I'm not joking. You really need to hurry.* Evan's panic was real. He could see the evil intent in Tamil's gaze.

"Once I've torn out Bleidd's heart, we can be together, and I'll give you everything he took away."

Evan's gums itched as his teeth grew at Tamil's threat. He knew Tamil could see his transformation. There was no hiding the way his eyes changed along with his body. "Once you do what?" Even Evan heard the preternatural growl to his voice.

Tamil didn't look worried. In fact, he eyed Evan like he couldn't wait to fuck him in wolf form. Rage filled Evan, making his skin tighten. "When he's dead, I'll bend you over his body and you can shoot your cum on the skin that once rejected you. Would you—"

A flash of surprise was all the reaction Tamil managed before Evan's jaw clamped down on his larynx, cutting off his words. The door exploded behind them. Evan twisted, feeling the shifter's windpipe crack beneath his teeth. Hot blood splashed Evan's face and filled his mouth. Nothing penetrated his thoughts beyond protecting his mate. This beast had draped Evan's mate in silver. Tried ending his life. Everything slowed. Tamil scrambled backward, clutching at the place where his throat should be. Evan spit, trying to separate himself from the monster who meant them harm. He felt no guilt. All that mattered was keeping Bleidd safe. Tamil fell to the floor with a loud thump. Bleidd's shocked expression went fuzzy. Darkness crowded the edges of his vision. Evan tried to stand. He felt nothing. His gaze dropped to his legs, convinced they were missing. Blood coated his clothes, turning them half red and half brown. A large pool of blood surrounded his feet. For some reason, the puddle got closer. Then, there was nothing.

## 8

Bleidd couldn't take his eyes off Evan. He was scared if he looked away, the man would disappear again. Bleidd hadn't worried about Evan as he should. His issues with the real Riskel were personal, going back hundreds of years. When he'd shown up in New Orleans, Bleidd had thought to pay Riskel some money and be done with their ancient feud, since he intended to claim his mate and stay here. Tamil wasn't even a blip on Bleidd's radar. Otherwise, he would've guarded his mate closely. Taking Riskel's identity had been a stroke of genius, since Bleidd had issues with both men. It had almost cost Evan his life. Now, even as Evan showered, Bleidd couldn't leave him in peace. He couldn't let Evan out of his sight. Water ran down Evan's beautiful body, washing Tamil's blood away.

Several times, Evan turned his face toward the deluge and filled his mouth before spitting it on the floor, as if he couldn't rid himself of the taste of almost killing someone. If Jonathan hadn't arrived and saved Tamil, he would be dead. Evan wasn't the type of person who could live with something like that.

The ache that started in Bleidd's chest when Baptiste informed him Evan was missing tripled. Nothing bad or unclean was ever supposed to touch Evan. It was his job to keep Evan safe from those things. Evan was too quiet. Even his mind was blank. Bleidd stripped. The need to hold Evan was making him antsy. When he tossed aside his final piece of clothing, Evan turned. His gaze ate Bleidd alive. All the wild colors that lived constantly inside Evan's head fired back to life as Bleidd stepped inside the shower. He watched Evan go hard. Bleidd's mouth watered.

*I've lived a long time. Seen and done so many things. Never have I encountered anyone like you.*

"Is that a good or a bad thing?" Evan asked aloud as if he didn't want to let Bleidd completely inside his head.

"It's amazing. You're amazing. Strong and brave. Gorgeous." Bleidd wrapped Evan in his arms and the man's hurt hit him, washing through Bleidd's thoughts, and drowning him. He could take it. Evan didn't deserve it. "It should've been me saving you. You should've waited for me. There should never be any spots on your soul."

Evan shook his head against Bleidd's chest. "He planned to kill you and... other things. I couldn't have that. No one is allowed to hurt you. I didn't mean to hurt him."

Bleidd's arms tightened around Evan. Evan was too good to be real, but Bleidd knew exactly what "other things" Tamil had planned for Evan, and he couldn't live with that. Tamil had been tainted long ago by a vampire who'd taken him in, forcing Tamil to trade sexual favors for survival. It was another stain on Bleidd's soul. One of many. It was also one of the reasons Bleidd had no problem walking away from leading the pack in Sweden. He'd been forced to make decisions for the greater good. Decisions that haunted him. Part of him wanted to find wherever Jonathan had Tamil stashed, and rip him to shreds for touching Evan. Another part of him wished he could go back in time and save Tamil before his soul turned to dust. That was the problem with life. No one knew where their decisions would lead until it was too late and there was nothing left but regret. "You have a warrior's heart," he said, hoping to keep Evan from the ugliness inside his head.

Light kisses brushed his collarbone, stirring Bleidd's body. He couldn't resist his mate. "You don't have to say that. I know I'm not a fighter. It's just that he threatened you. I saw red."

It wasn't right or fair to use the situation to dig for more affection from Evan, but Bleidd wasn't always good. In truth, he was a bad person more often than not. "Why?"

Evan tilted his chin up and met Bleidd's gaze. "What do you mean 'why'?"

Bleidd shrugged. "If he'd killed me, you'd be free." Bleidd stroked the small of Evan's back as he pointed out the obvious, because he couldn't stop touching Evan in every way. But, also, because once the words were out there, Bleidd realized how much he needed Evan to deny them. He needed to hear Evan say he wanted this. That being with Bleidd wasn't only about fate.

Evan licked his lips, looking nervous. "It would kill me if you died."

Bleidd couldn't stop. "Why?"

A line appeared between Evan's brows. He shook his head. "Why do you have to steal everything from me? You're not too good to bare your soul too, you know?"

Despite Evan's annoyance, a bright smile pulled at Bleidd's lips. "And you say you're not a warrior." Evan huffed and tried pulling away. Bleidd tightened his hold on Evan, refusing to let him get away. "I love you." Once the words were out there, Bleidd realized how easy they were to say. He shuffled Evan back against the shower wall. Possessiveness roared through him. Evan stared up at him, so trusting and hopeful. Bleidd dipped his head and lightly brushed his lips over Evan's. "I love you," he repeated, sounding firmer this time. "I fell in love with your every crazy thought four years ago and haven't shaken you since. Even if fate hadn't led me to you, I would've found you. I wouldn't have been able to stay away forever. You mean too much." Bleidd inched lower, kissing Evan's jaw, throat, and chest. After dropping to his knees, Bleidd nipped at Evan's stomach before licking the water from his skin. "So in love with you," he said again, incapable of not saying it now that the words were out there. Evan's cock stood proud, waiting for Bleidd's attention. While on his knees, Bleidd held Evan's stare.

Evan stroked his face. "I love you too."

At Evan's confession, Bleidd's eyes fell closed.

The words felt better than he'd ever imagined, especially coming from Evan. The boy couldn't know how much Bleidd needed someone to love him. Not because he was a leader, but because he was worthy of love. Bleidd wasn't sure that was true. He didn't think he deserved a damn thing, but he wanted Evan's affection.

Evan's fingers swiped through his hair. "Are you on your knees for a reason? I have to say, I'm not used to seeing you like this yet and it's kind of freaking me out. How long were you an alpha? Has anyone ever seen you on your knees? You know, you've never answered me any of the times I've asked you how old you are. If you're really, really old, your knees will be killing you soon."

A snort escaped Bleidd. His shoulders shook as he tried holding back his laughter. He wrapped his arms around Evan's waist, buried his face against the man's stomach, and let his laughter fly. Evan was priceless. When he was happy, he never shut up. The man had no idea how his every question proved how guileless he was.

Evan held Bleidd's head to his stomach while Bleidd laughed it out. "I like your laugh. You should do it more often. Maybe you could do it from a standing position. I'd like for you to still be able to walk tomorrow."

Bleidd turned his head and licked Evan's crown, killing the man's constant chatter. Evan sucked in an audible breath. Driven by the sound, Bleidd opened his mouth over Evan's cock, taking the man down his throat. He needed their love to wash away the taint of the world.

"Holy hell."

Bleidd might've started laughing again at Evan's curse if Bleidd wasn't so turned on. He could feel what Evan felt. His dick leaked onto the shower floor. He'd spent so much time hot for Evan's body, all Bleidd wanted to do was spend the rest of his life reveling in his mate. Bleidd craved showing Evan everything. He didn't hold back or take things slow. Bleidd sucked and licked, hollowing out his cheeks and taking Evan down his throat while setting a pace guaranteed to bring the man release. Evan clawed at his shoulders and tugged on his hair. Loud pants and moans bounced off the walls of the shower. Evan's hips moved, as if he couldn't control himself. Bleidd toyed with Evan's balls and asshole, openly fucking the man with his fingers.

Evan's entire body tensed. Triumph roared through Bleidd. A shout rent the air as hot cum filled Bleidd's mouth. Bleidd shot to his feet and covered Evan's mouth with his. Their tongues tangled as Bleidd stroked every last wave of pleasure from Evan. His heart overflowed with emotion. Soon, he would take his wolf to bed and claim his body. In a matter of moments, they would be one again. This man was the greatest treasure Bleidd had ever gained. He would never take Evan for granted. As he savored Evan's kiss, Bleidd made a silent vow. For the rest of eternity, Bleidd would nurture Evan's inner beauty, giving him the love he needed to thrive. Bleidd would spend every day until the end of time, thanking Odin for his perfect mate.

KEEP AN EYE OUT FOR BOOK #6, ACHE.

## ABOUT THE AUTHOR

Charity Parkerson is an award winning and multi-published author with several companies. Born with no filter from her brain to her mouth, she decided to take this odd quirk and insert it in her characters.

*Seven-time Readers' Favorite Award Winner

    *2015 Passionate Plume Award Finalist

    *2013 Reviewers' Choice Award Winner

    *2012 ARRA Finalist for Favorite Paranormal Romance

    *Five-time winner of The Mistress of the Darkpath

Connect with her online:

--Join my street team: facebook.com/TeamCharityParkerson

    --Sign up for my newsletter: http://bit.ly/CharityNews

--Website: charityparkerson.com
--Facebook: facebook.com/authorCharityParkerson
facebook.com/TheMenofSin
--Twitter: twitter.com/CharityParkerso